Decaf-A-Nation

by

Joanna Moore

Decaf-A-Nation

For Starfish

Chapter 1: A West Coast Departure

Marie rolled an oversized suitcase into the space designated for the handicap area, hoping no handicapped person would actually come by. She dropped her carry-on into the seat next to her. Her purse she rested on her lap. She was on the 5:45 a.m. light-rail train headed for the airport. It was still dark and the rain gave the cobblestone streets a soft glow. Marie leaned toward the window to see past her reflection and the train platform outside; no one was left in the darkness.

This slender, athletic woman stuck out as an oddity in Portland, Oregon, where the weather of the last six months had been overcast and rainy. Her light brown hair was visibly lightened from spending time in the sun and her skin had taken on a warm glow from regular exposure to it. Marie spent most of her time on the coast, and it is somewhat of a secret that the clouds actually part there in winter. It is also a little known fact that if you spend enough time on a surfboard on a cloudy day in January—even in the Northwest regions of the Pacific—you will eventually get a tan. This happened regularly enough to Marie that she was often mistaken for a tourist from Southern California.

Marie had called the Pacific Northwest her home for the last nine years. Most recently she had been working with local communities to protect the health of the ocean on behalf of Surfers of the Sea (SOS). She was particularly good at her job because she had an uncanny ability to read other people's emotions. This gave her the capacity to connect with strangers, see the world from their perspective, and use those insights to communicate with others about her own.

She had learned to do this from observing the ocean: the moods, the momentum, and the velocity of waves and currents. The way she learned to read the energy in the water was the same way in which she learned to read the energy of people. She picked up on their body language, ferreting out their fears and frustrations, as well as their desires—both fulfilled and unfulfilled.

Marie did not always work for SOS. She previously had a career at the Federal Bureau of Alcohol, Tobacco, Firearms & Explosives (commonly known as ATF). She had been stationed in the Seattle Field Division, traveling throughout Washington, Oregon, Alaska, Idaho and Hawaii for her work. Marie had been a special agent—a law enforcement officer trained to investigate and deal with drug-related activities. After years of this job she burned out. Her mind and body were tired of the ugliness she was seeing on a daily basis. The drug use, the violence, the trafficking and human exploitation. Hoping to find solace in nature and the sea, Marie started to volunteer for SOS. Within a year she found herself working for the organization and had left her old job behind.

Now Marie was leaving the West Coast. She was flying out to Charleston, South Carolina for a new position with Surfers of the Sea. This time she would be helping to protect the Atlantic from offshore drilling. The Southern Atlantic coast was slated for an ocean planning process to determine who could use the ocean and how. Many interests would be vying for a piece, including the oil and gas industry. For years this industry had pressured the federal government to allow offshore drilling in the region. A long-standing moratorium prevented this from happening. But every presidential election threatened to upend the moratorium. And now things were looking politically unwell. It was a constant political battle to keep the Atlantic ocean safe.

She had pondered all of this the previous day on her last surfing trip to the Pacific Ocean. Marie had paddled out and situated her board in deep water. It was early morning on a weekday and hardly anyone was around. A group of sea lions swam back and forth in front of her, keeping her company as she glued her eyes on the horizon. She absentmindedly felt the waves pass her by, and leapt over them with a surrendering grace as they reached her surfboard. She rose and sank against the surface of the water for what must have been an hour.

Eventually a feeling nudged at her that it was time to go. Her attention snapped back to her surroundings and she realized that the sea lions had disappeared. She looked around for them, regretting that she had not noticed their departure. Rather than leaving, however, they had lined themselves up some fifty yards behind her. They leapt over a wave like synchronized swimmers in the same manner she had been doing. Marie considered this to be their farewell to her.

***

The train now plodded slowly through downtown Portland, stopping at Pioneer Square. The doors opened, blasting in cold, damp morning air. Men in beanie hats and heavy utility gloves were setting up barricades in the plaza for an outdoor event. Early shift workers piled off of the train to start their day. The only person to board on was an old man with the dimensions of a garden gnome. He wore an orange reflective vest and carried a walking cane covered entirely with colorful rubber bands. Marie imagined him to be an old Russian immigrant from some place she had never heard of. He sat down across the aisle from her, closed his eyes, and became as motionless as a stone.

The train moved again, passing the urban scene outside slowly. The world was illuminated by the occasional street lamp and Marie had the sensation that they were moving through a doll house. It was the emptiness of the sidewalks and the scale of the buildings with their empty windows that gave her the impression. In a few more stops they reached a part of town that was animated with people again. A short pasty guy with salt-and-pepper hair got on the train with a bicycle. He headed straight for the handicap area next to Marie, obliging her to try to move her luggage out of the way.

"How's it going?" He asked behind aviator sunglasses, pushing the front wheel of his bike toward her kneecaps.

Marie noticed that he was jittery and his face was twitchy. "Fine, thanks," she responded, trying to steer clear of his bike. She

wondered whether he might be strung out on something—
possibly meth, as it was a known street drug in Portland. Being
observant about others was an old habit from her days at ATF.

"Thanks for making room for my bike; I take it with me
wherever I go. I've had a lot of bikes stolen from me in this
town." His voice felt abrupt in the early morning of the train.
"I'm usually not awake at this hour but I've got an early
appointment with my shrink. And I just had four shots of
espresso so hopefully I'll appear normal to her."   He leaned the
bike against Marie's luggage and sat down in an empty seat next
to the garden gnome.

Marie blinked a few times. She couldn't imagine what this guy
thought was normal.

"Where are you going? Hawaii?" Asked the biker.

"Ah…No…." The words left her mouth reluctantly and she
wondered how to escape this conversation. She decided not to
say anything further and settled on staring out the window.

The biker seemed let down and possibly hoped to find someone else to talk to. He stood up and moved back into the aisle near the doors. "Look at all this new development!" He shouted to no one and everyone at once, motioning to the high-rises across the river. "Buildings going up all over the city! They should build a 200 story building, don't you think?"

There were a few other people still in the train car, but no one responded. The garden gnome kept his eyes closed and did not move. The lack of response perplexed the bike guy, who took out a cigarette and pushed it between his lips, waiting for the opportunity to light it.

They plodded for some time in silence until the train stopped across the river. The biker pulled his bike away from Marie's luggage and exited through the nearest doors. She watched as he sped away across the sidewalk.

They accelerated along the highway, leaving the center of town behind. The gnome-like figure in the safety vest across from her started to snore. Marie turned her attention toward the window again. She could see garbage in the brush and occasional encampments of homeless people in the gulches they passed by.

These encampments were growing more common. The newspapers were talking about the homeless and everyone in town kept saying that someone should do something about it. But no one ever did.

The encampments eventually disappeared from view and were replaced by a cluster of modern buildings and billboards. Those ultimately gave way to trees and darkness. Marie watched the scenery for a while until her eyes could no longer stay open.

Half an hour later the train stopped abruptly at the airport, causing Marie to jerk her head up. She realized that she must have drifted into sleep. A rough voice with a stunning New Jersey accent spoke next to her: "Well, after all that, he's forgotten his lock." It was the gnome in the safety vest, looking at a bike lock in the seat next to him; it must have belonged to the biker. The gnome heaved himself up onto his cane and departed for the airport. Marie gathered her belongings and followed behind him.

Chapter 2: Two Hearts Coffee

Two days later, Marie was getting oriented in Charleston. Surfers of the Sea had arranged a meeting for her with Sean Bianchi, owner of a local real estate development company that invested in properties along South Carolina's coast. Sean was very welcoming to Marie and had a lot of useful information to share about local coastal politics. He also had experience with government planning workshops like the one that was just about to begin in Charleston around the future of the Atlantic Ocean.

It turned out that Sean was also a personal friend of Roman Ferrari, the Italian tennis player who had won Wimbledon the previous year. Roman was an avid windsurfer with a passion for clean oceans. Based on that passion, Sean had invited Roman to an Oil Free Oceans event that the South Carolina Chapter of Surfers of the Sea was hosting in a few weeks. Roman had agreed enthusiastically not only to attend the event but also be featured in an SOS video against offshore drilling.

Marie left the meeting with a feeling of confidence regarding her work on the offshore drilling campaign. She walked through downtown Charleston with exuberance and a childlike curiosity for the town she had yet to explore. Now strolling through the streets of Charleston's French Quarter, Marie admired the old buildings with their wrought iron gates, intricate balconies, and decorative stucco. Her eyelids softened as she moved through the dappled light of the palm trees lining the sidewalk.

The streets became narrower and the buildings around her looked even older and more softly worn. She stopped at an intersection and looked around gingerly. Street noises had faded and myrtle trees fluttered in the wind. The air pressure had changed somewhat as well. She knew she was close to water—possibly just a few blocks away from Charleston Harbor.

Marie decided to walk into a coffee shop across the street. She was drawn to its open, tall windows, which let the breeze in from the outside. She entered confidently, assessing the space. Her attention was drawn to a series of photos of North Atlantic right whales bathing in glassy ocean waves. She then admired a collage of the various islands and land formations that make up the City of Charleston. It was abstracted from cut-outs of newspaper articles, with each chunk roughly suggesting a street or long row of houses.

Marie studied the map until she sensed that the barista behind the counter was observing her. He may have been looking at her for quite some time now; she realized. "I like your place," she acknowledged him with a warm smile.

"Thank you; my brother and I have run this coffee shop for almost three years now. I'm Brigg." He smiled back at her.

"I'm Marie. Nice to meet you." He was wearing a thick cotton shirt with a soft texture that Marie wanted to touch. It was blue, with a subtle pattern of beige in it.

"Are you touring Charleston?" Brigg asked, after assessing that there was no one behind her in line.

"Oh, I just moved here. I've been with Surfers of the Sea on the Pacific Coast; and now I'm working on the Atlantic."

Brigg looked at Marie with curiosity. "I know SOS. I've seen the North Carolina chapter's Facebook page—with all the pictures of people holding signs protesting offshore drilling? That's pretty powerful stuff."

Brigg was quite tan and Marie wondered whether he spent a great deal of time on the water. "That's what I'll be working on. Have you heard of the South Atlantic Ocean Planning process that's beginning here in Charleston? One of the hot topics will be whether to allow offshore drilling." Answered Marie.

"I haven't heard about any offshore drilling plans. That would suck; royally. I'm glad you're here working on it, though." He replied.

"Thanks!" She answered and then changed topics. "I love those whale prints; they're beautiful." She pointed across the cafe.

Brigg turned to the photos appreciatively. "My friend Sydney took those. He runs tour boats up the coast. You should talk to him—maybe he can help you." Brigg reached over into a drawer and pulled out his card. "Here's my contact info; email me and I'll connect you to Sydney."

"I appreciate it." Marie took his card. She then looked up at the list of daily roasts, neatly handwritten on an overhead chalkboard.

"If you like a darker roast, I recommend the Chat Noir. Think roasted hazelnut, cherries, and chocolate. If you prefer a light roast, I recommend the Morning Merengue. It has some creamy citrus overtones." Offered Brigg.

"I'll go with the Chat Noir—small Americano, please. I don't do the lighter roasts—the flavors are too weird for me." Stated Marie.

"I can't do the lighter roasts either, honestly. But my brother's into them." Brigg grabbed a tapered ceramic mug and worked the espresso machine. "You must get some good surf on the West Coast." He commented over the whine of the steamer.

"They've got some good waves. It can be a bit choppy and soupy at times in Oregon, though." Offered Marie. "How about here?" She sized Brigg up as a potential surfer.

"It's not too bad. My brother and I surf over at Folly Beach when we can't get out of town—which is most of the time. There should be some good days over there this week." He handed her the coffee.

***

"Aren't you Roman Ferrari?" Asked Brigg soon after Marie had left the cafe.

"Yes; and this is my wife, Gabriella." The charismatic athlete introduced his equally athletic and charismatic spouse. "Are you a tennis fan?"

"I'm Brigg. Brigg Kelley. My brother Tom plays doubles at the Charleston Tennis Center. He's a big fan of yours." Responded Brigg. "What are the two of you doing in South Carolina?"

"I am playing a tournament at the Savage Beach Resort. And my wife is teaching a tennis workshop over there." Roman gladly accepted his cappuccino from Brigg.

***

"Did you see that, Chris? That's Roman Ferrari!" Exclaimed Tucker Watts to Chris Buckley as they grabbed a corner table inside the coffee shop.

"That's that guy in the espresso machine ads." Observed Chris, frowning.

"No; Roman Ferrari is a tennis player. He's a tennis champion." Responded Tucker while craning his neck to observe Roman navigate past some tables.

"Yeah, well he's also the guy in the espresso machine ads." Insisted Chris. "I've seen them on YouTube. With the dancing robot who puts away his tennis rackets. Luca, I think. It's on the top ten lists of the most expensive espresso makers on the planet.

Tucker looked at Chris, trying to follow the story line. "Why are you watching espresso machine ads on YouTube?"

"They run on occasion." Chris answered crustily. He then turned his head toward Ferrari. "He's probably going over to the resort to play tennis and drink coffee out of one of those precious machines." Chris's annoyance turned to sulking and he began spinning his coffee mug around on the table.

Tucker stared at Chris blankly for a moment. "Who cares what he's doing?"

Chris did not appear to have heard the question. "Another coffee-drinking asshole. He's staring at that map of Charleston like he's planning to buy his second or third home here. This town's already infested with latte drinking computer geeks and hipsters buying up entire neighborhoods. Soon enough I won't be able to afford to live here. I'll have to share a house with some guy who wears metal washers for earrings."

"But you're here drinking coffee, too. And so am I. What's wrong with drinking coffee, anyway?" Asked Tucker.

"Nothing." Said Chris, crossing his arms and growing resentfully calm. "But it costs three dollars in a place like this. And that's just messed up."

"It's pour-over." Tucker tried to move on. "He's probably trying to figure out how to get to the Isle of Palms. Maybe he's playing a match at the Savage Beach Resort." Tucker got up and stretched his back, eyeing to get Roman's autograph.

"Isle of Palms…" Chris nearly spat out. "Why doesn't he come by Jameson Island where the rest of us live? He probably won't see a thing of this town except that damn tennis resort."

"Well, what do you want to do, kidnap him because he's not here to visit Jameson Island?" Asked Tucker, mockingly waving his arms over Chris.

Chris sat thinking, arms folded and leaning back in his seat. "We could mix a little something into the coffee blend they serve at the Savage Beach Resort. My cousin Jamie does research into tobacco mold at Demson University. That would improve Roman's coffee experience in Charleston tremendously."

Tucker rolled his eyes and walked over to get an autograph from Roman.

Chapter 3: Kitty Hawk

A week later on a breezy morning in April, Marie stood on the beach in Kitty Hawk, North Carolina. The view was endless ocean and sand. Water swirled and foamed under an overcast sky and the wind blew heavy chunks of her wet hair onto her cheeks. She and her companion had just carried surfboards out of the water and set them down on the beach. Both of them breathed heavily after paddling back in to shore. Few surfers were out on the ocean, as tourist season had not yet started. And the sun shone thinly at this early hour, attracting only the more dedicated surfers from the surrounding community of Kitty Hawk.

The two settled their feet into soft sand and gazed back out to sea. Jeff Hardy was shorter than Marie, slightly stalky, with dark brown hair and skin tanned to the color of chocolate pudding. He was the president of the North Carolina Chapter of SOS. His sister lived in Charleston and Marie was staying in her guest bedroom until she could find an apartment.

"Over to the North over there is where they wanted to set up the drilling operations," He explained, pointing across his chest and outward to sea.

"No way!" Exclaimed Marie. "That's just about as ridiculous as setting up a mining operation in the middle of Yellowstone Park. Did anyone take them seriously?"

"The feds, mostly." Noted Jeff bitterly. "Everyone else was up in arms. This place is the number one tourist destination on the coast. None of the businesses or residents would stand for it."

"How much oil do they think is here anyway?" Asked Marie.

"The numbers the feds provide state that between Florida and New Jersey there is less than a year's worth of oil to fuel US demand." Jeff squinted his eyes toward the horizon and folded his arms across his chest.

"Then why are they even bothering?" Asked Marie incredulously. "That sounds like a drop in the bucket in the grand scheme of things. And why pursue this location so aggressively? I mean, if you are trying to get approval for offshore drilling along the coast, why not pick somewhere less desirable as a tourist destination? Why pick the Outer Banks?"

Jeff scratched his chin. "Well, they have been wanting to conduct seismic testing out here for some time to map out the oil and gas reserves. But because of the endangered species issues— with the North Atlantic right whales and dolphins and so forth— they haven't been able to get a permit. But they might have some insider knowledge that they are going to find a boatload of oil here. We suspect there are some military documents they got a hold of suggesting this area is worth their time. You know, the military does things we don't hear about. They may have already evaluated this area decades ago for oil and gas reserves."

"If there is any document about reserves in the Atlantic that we haven't seen, then we definitely need to get a hold of it." Marie announced with determination. "Someone in the public sector must have a copy. Otherwise why would the feds be taking these guys so seriously?"

"You've got a point there," Jeff turned to Marie. "That might explain why the feds were so accommodating to these guys. We'll do what we can on our end, but you might have better luck getting a hold of any military surveys during the planning workshops down in Charleston. The big wigs will be coming into town and they can't ignore you as much if you are standing right in front of them." He now looked at Marie with a combination of hope and pity. "You're going to need some luck, I think."

***

Marie was back in South Carolina a week later. She had biked out to a fly fishing shop in Mount Pleasant, a suburb of Charleston, to meet Sydney, the whale photographer. She now sorted through her bag and pulled out her new business card. It read, Marie Alpen, South Atlantic Regional Manager, Surfers of the Sea.

Butterflies began dancing in her stomach again as she wondered how she could claim that title knowing so little about the region. She had taken five days to drive back from Kitty Hawk along the coast, touring first up and down the Outer Banks, then making her way through the communities and nature reserves between North and South Carolina. She had a list of ocean-friendly businesses with her, which had been put together by an SOS intern the prior year. Marie roughly estimated that she had managed to visit at most about 5% of the businesses on her list. Her thoughts were interrupted when a guy with a square jaw and trucker cap came out of the back room. "I heard you were looking for me?" He asked.

"Sydney? I'm Marie. Your friend Brigg told me to look you up about your photos of the Atlantic right whales at his cafe. I work for Surfers of the Sea, but I'm not very familiar with this coastline. I was transferred recently from the Pacific Northwest to help protect the Southern Atlantic from offshore drilling." She handed Sydney her card.

He took the card with a modicum of surprise and gazed at it for a while. "I didn't know there were any plans for offshore drilling around here. I thought that was something they only did in the Gulf of Mexico."

"There are powerful interests working on getting access to the Atlantic. There's going to be a series of government workshops in the coming months around the use of this part of the coast. We want to make sure it gets protected." Replied Marie.

"Why are you interested in me?" He asked, looking both modest and slightly surprised.

"Well, you know something about the right whales. I'm hoping that could help." She responded.

"I know the whales migrate down here in the winter and give birth to their young along the Carolinas and Georgia. There are only 400 or so right whales left in total—a quarter of them are females in their reproductive years." Sydney reported. He then paused and looked like he tasted something slightly bitter in his mouth. "Sometimes I tell people that and they ask me, why bother? Why is it worth saving them?"

"What do you tell them?" Marie was wide-eyed with curiosity.

"Why would you not save them? It makes people uncomfortable when I ask that because they realize they don't have an answer. Not a very good answer, at least." He stretched his chest. "I used to tell people the whales are an important part of the ecosystem. But that did't make much of an impression. I could see most people's eyes glazing over. So now I just show them the photos and talk about what it's like to be so close to whales. That always gets people excited. Speaks to their hearts — not their anxieties about their mortgage."

"What is it like — to be around the whales, I mean?" Marie followed Sydney's train of thought.

He leaned his hand on a metal display rack of high performance sunscreen. "It's pretty amazing." His face softened. "You see their eyes, and they are alert, yet quite calm. You know there is a soul behind those eyes — an intelligent being thinking and feeling. They just don't happen to speak our language. You feel their size and their power, yet they move slowly around you and are quite gentle. Like they are guarding you or working gently to connect with you."

"It must be an amazing experience," Marie murmured to him.

"It is." Sydney agreed. "And really, unless you get in there with them under water (which I never did) you are just scratching the surface. There is a whole world under that surface that they inhabit. They mostly get exposed to human civilization through helicopters and boats. It is rare that whales and humans actually get up close to each other."

"I wonder what they think of us," mused Marie.

Sydney looked at her matter-of-factly for a moment, and then sniffed his nose. "I had a dream about that once. That I was out in the water talking to them. They told me that humans get lost in their technologies. That our cars and our boats are like armor from the rest of the world and sever our ability to perceive and care for nature."

Marie lowered her eyes for a moment, feeling the regret behind Sydneys last statement. Then she looked up kindly. "Sydney? How would you feel about sharing your experiences again with another audience?"

Chapter 4: Tobacco Mold

Chris walked toward the Demson University Pee Dee Research and Education Center. This was the place his cousin Jamie Buckley liked to call his home away from home. Jamie had always made fun of the kids who had ambitions to go to college, until his dad encouraged him to get a higher education. Jamie took on the challenge, and began researching ways of tying his love for the family farm to the most obscure and academic pursuit he could locate within South Carolina.

This turned out to be at the Agricultural and Environmental Sciences Department at Demson University. Jamie obtained his Bachelor's in Agricultural Biotechnology and stayed on to pursue advanced degrees through lab and field research into tobacco. The work suited him well because it gave him an opportunity to escape into the lab when he was particularly annoyed or frustrated with the world. At the same time, it allowed him to maintain a presence in the agricultural fields of Darlington County.

Chris walked into the main building of the Pee Dee Research Center purposefully, thinking about his cousin Jamie, and continued down a hallway to pause near a locked door. He fumbled with his cell phone until an employee he had followed from the parking lot opened the door with a security code. "Oh, thanks." He mumbled to the disappearing figure and grabbed the door.

He hadn't visited his cousin at the lab since Jamie first started working there. He got a peek inside when he helped Jamie move some equipment for Jamie's research project. Chris knew his visit now would not be well received.

He walked down the next hallway looking for signs that would refresh his memory about the location of his cousin's workspace. After some false starts, he hit upon a door with a window through which he could see Jamie's silhouette. He paused, took a deep breath, and rapped sharply on the window. His cousin startled and jerked up.

Jamie's look of surprise turned into confusion and slight apprehension as he walked to the door and recognized Chris' face pressed up against the glass. "What are you doing here, Chris? How did you even get in?" He asked in a half whisper as he swung the door open.

Chris pushed his body forward and let himself in before Jamie could step out into the hallway. "Hey, Jamie, what's goin' on, bud? I haven't been here forever! How are the mold spores doing?" He surveyed the lab space expectedly.

At the end of a table near where Jamie had been perched on a high stool lay stacks of sorted petri dishes. Chris moved instinctively toward them, then turned around toward Jamie with a big smile. "Have you finally developed the perfect cheese in this place?"

"Ha, ha. Very funny, Chris. What are you doing here?" Jamie was not at all amused.

"I didn't mean to bother you like this, Jamie. But I knew if I called you, you'd say no." Chris realized he didn't have much of a game plan for snagging some mold once he got in to see Jamie. He stalled for time, looking around the lab. "What do you do with this?" He picked up a beaker and nearly dropped it.

"Watch it, Chris; those don't grow on trees!" Jamie rushed to the rescue.

"Sorry bud! Jamie rearranged the beaker on the table like
someone would rearrange a bouquet of flowers.

"Chris, why are you here?" Jamie crossed his arms and waited
grimly. His cousin had been there for him on many occasions
when Jamie needed to make things happen. But he could also be
careless and stupid, like when he threw a milkshake out the car
window at oncoming traffic or when he told Jamie's girlfriend
that her German Shepherd had been run over by a car as a
practical joke. He stood there waiting, not knowing what was
coming.

Chris could only think of one thing he could say to Jamie that
would dampen any suspicion about his real motive: he would
have to ask Jamie for money. A thought started to form in his
mind. "Look. Bud, I'll get right to the point." He stopped and
grasped around for a good story.

"Well?" Jamie looked at him, waiting for an explanation.

Finally, an idea crossed Chris' mind. "I'm going to lose my
boating license real fast if I don't cough up five hundred bucks in
the next day or two." The words blurted out of Chris' mouth.

Jamie tried to get his pupils to focus on his cousin. "What do you mean?" He managed to say.

"Five hundred dollars." Chris cleared his throat. "Look, Bud, I need your help. You don't need to know all the details and you probably don't want to, anyway. I went out on the water a little drunk the other night and hit one of those mini yachts outside of Charleston Harbor. I was real apologetic, but the guy was pissed. I promised I'd handle it right away so that the insurance company wouldn't get involved. You know how they are. They'd ask around and find out I'd been drinking."

"What are you doing drinking and getting in that boat? You could kill someone!" Exclaimed Jamie.

"I know, really bad decision. I am definitely not going to do that again. Look Bud, it wouldn't be fair for me to take the heat for it like this. I need that boat; it's my livelihood. I can't work at that damn tennis resort forever." Chris was looking wildly around the room, trying to calculate how he was going to get a petri dish of mold into his possession without his cousin noticing.

Jamie started pacing, agitated. "So you do something crazy like this and then you show up asking for help. It's one thing to pull your motorcycle out from the reeds or help clean up after one of your parties. But to give you money to pay off some guy..." He was no longer looking at Chris.

And Chris had stopped listening. Instead he gently fingered toward the petri dishes on the main lab table, and noiselessly managed to lift one and put it in his back pocket. A feeling of serenity and satisfaction came over him. He waited until his cousin was finished. "Okay Bud, I know you are right. Look, I can probably scrape up a couple hundred, but the other three hundred is a no go. I will take responsibility for what I can now, and pay you back later. Please, Bud."

Jamie stopped pacing and stood thoughtfully. Chris' calm demeanor diffused his feelings of agitation. He sighed sharply, which turned into a sniff. "Alright; I'll loan you the money. But I want it back soon."

"Thanks Jamie—you're a good guy. I truly appreciate this," Chris offered with a broad smile.

"Okay—okay, now you've got to go," responded Jamie, looking at the clock, "my boss is due in a few minutes." Chris was already halfway out the door and waiving before Jamie had finished the sentence. He was gone as quickly as he came.

Jamie went back to his work space and sat down. He felt puzzled by his cousin's visit and had a vague sense that he had been duped somehow. He stared down at the petri dishes that had recently arrived on his desk from one of the other researchers. He started sorting them absentmindedly, wondering about his cousin's motivations.

A few minutes passed and the Principal Investigator for Jamie's research came through the door. John Warren was Jamie's boss and a distinguished professor at Demson. He was especially distinguished for keeping South Carolina's tobacco plants healthy, a task he successfully had managed for over thirty years. As a result, he had many friends in the tobacco industry who were major donors to Demson University and this particular lab. Jamie was his current favorite researcher and John hoped Jamie would continue the success of the lab.

John had some trepidation, however, regarding what would become of the lab and the potential he saw in Jamie. Tobacco just wasn't very popular any more. Sure, the Europeans were still smoking, and countries like Thailand seemed to go through cigarettes like nothing else. But the US market was on a steady decline. Laws across the country had outright banned smoking within buildings and lawsuits had cracked down hard on cigarette companies.

All of this had taken a toll on the South Carolina economy, and this was also reflected in donations to Demson University and the lab. Somehow they would have to reinvent themselves, and John was starting to feel the pressure.

Things were even more complicated because the University had recently announced financial losses in its employee retirement funds. Apparently the University had made some aggressive investments in high tech but hadn't cashed out before the last bubble burst. It would take years for those funds to recover. And John was pretty livid. After all these years of service, he was being left standing in the cold just moments away from retirement.

"What have we got here, Jamie?" John asked, pulling up a stool across from his junior.

"I've finally managed to turn the aggressive gene on and off in the lab culture. I have also been able to get the non-aggressive mold to reproduce with the aggressive mold on demand." Replied Jamie, pointing to the two sets of petri dishes on the table. "The question is whether it will be possible to scale this for agricultural use."

"So you're saying that you believe you can fight the aggressive form of tobacco mold by spraying the plants with the non-aggressive mold so that they will breed together?" Inquired John, lifting one petri dish to the light.

"That's right. Why use fungicides when you can use a Trojan horse to inoculate the mold?" Replied Jamie. "But currently the aggressive mold still holds the dominant gene, and results are varied with cross-breeding. The genes still need some tweaking."

"I see…." Said John, pokerfaced, and fell into silence for a moment. He then asked, "And you did use the derivative from the coffee mold to create the aggressive mold?"

"Yes, I incorporated it into the yeast culture and it developed nicely."

"Very good. Very good, Jamie." He said picking up one of the mold cultures. "This sounds like quite a promising way to go." He stood up and placed the culture back on the table. "Keep me updated on your progress."

***

At 5 am the following morning, John walked quietly into the Pee Dee Research Center. He grabbed a petri dish of coffee mold out of a refrigerator and took it to his work table. He turned on his computer and plugged it into a machine that looked like a glorified microscope. He then walked over to the coffee machine and gave it life while he waited for his computer and the microscope to talk to each other.

A few minutes later the coffee machine started to gurgle and black liquid poured into his mug. He added some creamer from the refrigerator and settled back into his seat.

While sipping his coffee, John flipped through the manual for the contraption. The "CRISPR Genome Editing Resource Guide: A Complete DNA Engineering Solution." There was a picture of a pair of scissors cutting into a double-helix diagram of DNA on the front cover. John refreshed his memory on the final steps of what exactly he wanted to do. He flipped back and forth between a couple of diagrams until he felt satisfied. He placed the DNA of the coffee mold in a centrifuge that resembled a top-load washer. His handiwork was magnified and projected onto his computer screen.

It was nearly 8 am when John finished. He carefully put the mold he had been working on in a small cooler. He turned off his computer and the glorified microscope. Washed his coffee mug and put it in the drying rack. He then took the mini cooler with the coffee mold and walked out of the building and back to his car. He drove the mold sample to his house and put it in a special freezer.

An hour later, John was back at the Pee Dee Research Center for his work day. Jamie was already working in one of the lab spaces and John popped in to see him. "Jamie?"

"Yes?" answered Jamie, looking up from his petri dishes.

"I am going to be traveling on vacation as of next week." John
stated.

Jamie looked up in surprise, not remembering John's plans.
"How long will you be gone?"

"Just a couple of weeks. I know it is a little last-minute. And I
haven't put it into the lab calendar yet. But I have a special
opportunity I want to take advantage of." He smiled at Jamie
with an angelic smile and gave him a wave as he exited the door.

Chapter 5: Savage Beach

It was a mild Saturday morning in Charleston when Chris and Tucker met up at an empty parking lot near the Arthur Ravenel Junior Bridge. Tucker pulled up in his white unmarked work van and parked beside Chris' black pick-up truck. Chris had been waiting for him outside, wearing his tennis club uniform: khaki pants and a light blue polo shirt with "Savage Beach" embroidered on the front. He was leaning on the back of his truck with his arms crossed. Unfolding himself, he approached the van and gave Tucker a warm greeting.

"Hey Tucker, glad you made it!" he exclaimed, slapping Tucker on the back. Moving over to the van, he gave it an appreciative pat. "This vehicle's going to be perfect."

Tucker chewed some tobacco thoughtfully. "You saw your cousin Jamie?"

"Yep; I certainly did. I near-about cracked up while I was in there. He got all worked up when I asked him for money." Chris was tickled.

"What money?" Tucker switched cheeks.

"I made up a story about bouncing off of a yacht and needing three hundred dollars. He got all uppity about my boating habits after that. That distracted him long enough that I could pocket a petri dish with one of his mold specimens." Chris explained.

"You gonna share that with me, or what?" Tucker pocketed his hands.

"The mold?" Chris asked innocently.

Tucker cracked a smile. "I mean the three hundred dollars; you want me to work for you, you've gotta contribute to my fishing fund."

"Aw, Tucker…come on! You know I'm broke! Why do you want to take that cash from me?"

"Fifty percent, Chris. And it's not your money; it's Jamie's." Tucker held out his hand expectedly."

Chris huffed. "I don't have it all here. I can give you fifty dollars." He pulled out his wallet and satisfied Tucker's outstretched palm.

"Thank you." Tucker accepted the counter-offer, putting the money away. "So how exactly do you want to do this?"

"Glad you asked, Bro." Chris, responded, and walked over to his truck. He unlatched the back gate to reveal a stuffed burlap sack the size of a large garbage bag. "I've got this special batch of coffee beans that I've been brewing with Jamie's mold right here. You deliver it in your van to the restaurant loading area, and I will meet you there. Then I'll mix these beans in with their coffee beans. It's that simple." He pulled the burlap sack out of the truck and plopped it unceremoniously onto the ground.

Tucker was still chewing. "Did you taste 'em?" He asked.

"What; the beans? Naw, I don't need to. They smell bad enough." Responded Chris. With that, he opened the sack and gestured Tucker to come closer and take a whiff.

Tucker leaned nose first into the sack of coffee beans. Not a moment later he jerked his head back up violently and started heaving. "Aw gad!" He spit out his tobacco, seriously at risk of choking on it. That's disgusting!" He let out a few coughs for good measure and made the sound of a cat about to sneeze. "That's effin moldy!"

"That's the idea!" Responded Chris with a smile. He turned to the task of closing up the burlap sack and stuffing it into Tucker's van. "You ready?" He asked. "I'm due to clock in soon."

"Ready as I'll ever be. I don't know how you ever talked me into this." Stated Tucker. With that, they got in their vehicles and headed for the Isle of Palms.

***

The following Monday morning, Julia Lockhart was sitting in her office at the Savage Beach Resort. She was waiting for the clock on her computer to strike 9 am so that she could call her coffee distributor and demand an explanation. It had been a horrible weekend.

First, the complaints about the taste and the smell of their coffee.
Then a number of their guests became ill. Nausea. Vomiting.
Cold sweats. All in the middle of a major tennis tournament and
fund raiser. As the lead manager responsible for guest
satisfaction, Julia took the heat. It was a total disaster. And she
was totally blind-sided. She had finally followed the trail back to
their coffee, and found that everything was tainted—a whole
month's supply smelled like rotten mold.

The clock finally turned 9, and Julia picked up the phone. She
dialed a number off of her computer screen and waited for a
reply.

"Kshhh...kszz..offee Distributors." Emerged a voice through the
static on the other end of the line. "For sales, press one; for
billing, press two..."

"Customer Service" announced Julia into the receiver, drumming
a pen against the edge of her desk.

"One moment please…" the voice on the other line was cut off
by a ring tone, followed by a transition into background music.

Julia breathed heavily into the receiver, and swung her chair away from the desk.

A man's voice on the other end abruptly cut into the music. "Did you know, our coffee is individually crafted around the world, and expertly blended to produce the finest notes…." The man's voice was suddenly cut off by a woman's voice, "Customer Service, this is Tony. How may I help you?"

"Hi Tony, this is Julia Lockhart. I'm the manager at the Savage Beach Resort in Charleston, South Carolina? We received a batch of moldy coffee beans last week from you that have made our guests sick and nearly shut us down this weekend. What is going on?"

"What is your account number, mam?" Asked Tony.

Julia let out another heavy breath into the receiver. "It's 4802 2454 70031."

There was silence on the other line. "Hello?" Asked Julia, thinking she may have lost the connection.

"I'm looking that up, mam." Said Tony on the other line. "Are you calling from Savage Beach Resort?"

"Yes," responded Julia, thinking how she had already said that.

"Our records show that your last delivery was this past Thursday," stated Tony.

"Yes, that's correct." Confirmed Julia.

"And what was the problem, mam?" Asked Tony.

Julia took a slow breath and looked out of a small window facing the beach. "As I mentioned," she began curtly, "the coffee we received was moldy. Some sort of toxic mold—every one of our guests who drank the coffee this weekend got sick."

"Where do you store your coffee, mam?" Asked Tony.

"Where do we store it? Where we've always stored it. What do you mean?" Responded Julia.

"If you store your coffee in humid conditions—maybe in a room that has mold in the walls—it may be possible for the mold to have tainted your coffee." Responded Tony.

Julia squinted her eyes and put her left hand to her temple. She felt heat rising up the back of her neck. "No, you're not getting this, Tony. This is an exclusive tennis resort, not a public housing slum. Your coffee arrived moldy, and we need a replacement as soon as possible."

"No one else has ever complained about this before," chimed Tony.

Julia took in a deep sharp breath and gathered her energies. "Don't try that 'no one else has ever complained about this before' garbage on me, Tony. I work in customer service too. I need you to get these beans out of here. Unless you want a bill for the damage."

"Right away, mam."

Chapter 6: The Yankee

Alexis Jones sat in her office on the sixth floor of a quaint building in downtown Charleston. She had a beautiful view of Charleston Harbor, glittering under the bobbing sailboats and blue sky. As with most mornings, this view was a distant abstraction to Alexis. Her attention was instead focused on a new project. The assignment came via email from Garett Bellingham, a senior partner who had an office one floor down from hers. Most of her interactions with Garett were by email. Indeed, she rarely saw him or even spoke on the phone to him. He was too busy to come by. Nevertheless, she usually received a short email from him every other week — just to confirm he was still alive, she imagined.

Alexis leaned toward the message in her inbox and opened the attachment again. It was an unusual project sent to Charleston from a law firm in New Jersey, asking Whyte, Farm & Bellingham to research the access rights to build oil docks and storage terminals for offshore drilling along the Atlantic coast. Normally this type of project would first be sent to a junior associate, but this one had a sense of urgency to it. And so it was forwarded to

Alexis because she was the most senior associate and was experienced enough to handle the matter on her own.

She did not like the idea of working on offshore drilling. Indeed, she was hoping to get more work on renewable energy projects. She already had one wind energy client assigned to her from another partner and had aspirations to develop a renewable energy practice. The oil client felt like a step in the wrong direction to her. With a deep sigh, Alexis got up from her desk and grabbed her mug. She headed to the break room to make herself an Americano from the firm's prized Luca Espresso Machine. She needed a boost of motivation to make this project work. And it was going to be a long week.

***

The following Monday morning, Alexis walked toward the reception desk at Whyte, Farm & Bellingham. The attorney she had corresponded with on the offshore drilling project was there from New Jersey and waiting for her in the conference room. She could see him through the glass separating the lobby from the meeting space. He wore a dark suit and sat with his elbows on the table, hands clenched together. His hair was neatly cropped and starting to grey. Even though he was slim, his face was slightly swollen from overwork and his eyes were puffy from lack of sleep.

"Steve Ledermeier?" Alexis asked, entering through the glass doors. "It is nice to meet you. I'm Alexis Jones; we spoke on the phone."

"Hello Alexis," Steve got up and shook her hand; Alexis' fingers felt crushed under the weight of his grasp.

"Garett is on his way." She managed to pull away her hand and recover feeling in her fingers. "Let me flag down the receptionist for some refreshments while we are waiting." With that, she stepped out the door. When she reappeared, she was joined by a dark-haired man with a permanent smile on his face. This was Garett Bellingham.

"Hi Steve, so good to see you again." Announced Garett, his cufflinks peeking through a blue sports jacket as he reached to shake Steve's hand.

"You always look the same, Garett," responded Steve. "Time has treated you well."

"It's the sailing, my friend. It keeps me young." Garett's smile got wider. The men took their seats across from each other and Alexis settled in next to Garett.

"I have to admit, I was a bit surprised to hear from you, Steve. Doesn't Kenny handle land use matters in your office?" Garett turned the conversation to work.

"Yes, well, Kenny won't be joining us." Steve looked down at the gloss of the conference table. "He passed away suddenly. Had a heart attack at the office late one night. There was no one around to take him to the hospital."

"Ohhhhh…..I'm so sorry, Steve. That's a terrible loss." Garett looked genuinely ashen.

"Thanks." Steve looked up and paused a few breaths to show Kenny his respect. Then he continued: "I took over the case because I'm doing some litigation work for CTG already. This is not my area of expertise, however. So I appreciate your help."

"We've taken a look at the issue, Steve. Your project is quite an ambitious one." Garett took the lead, speaking slowly.

"Yes, well it might be ambitious but this is what CTG wants." Responded Steve.

Garett and Alexis looked at each other. "They might know what they want, but they might have a very difficult time getting it." Responded Garett, adjusting his expensive watch.

Steve's face creased with mild irritation.

At that moment, the door behind Alexis and Garett opened. A plump woman in her sixties with peroxide blond hair came in with coffee and water. "I have coffee for you!" She announced, smiling at the three of them. Before anyone could react, she turned and headed to get more supplies out of a side cabinet.

"It's all right here in this memo," began Alexis and handed Steve a report the thickness of the tax code. "I've looked at the state, regional and local permit requirements on this, and..."

"Here we are!" Interjected the blond woman who was now ceremoniously laying out a tray of mugs and other items on the table.

"Thanks, Carol." Said Garett.

"You are very welcome, Garett. Enjoy!" Carol gave everyone another smile and promptly exited the conference room.

"Care for some coffee?" Asked Garett, reaching for a mug.

"Yes—thank you." Steve's eyes lit up.

"How about you, Alexis?" Asked Garett.

"Yes, please." She nodded enthusiastically.

Garett proceeded to fill three mugs while Alexis continued.

"Technically there are legal grounds for granting the permit." She explained. "But it is going to be politically unpopular—the agencies have discretion to deny such an application, and they are likely to use it."

Steve's facial color seemed to shift from pink to red. "Politically unpopular?" He repeated.

"Yes, well, as you know, the drill site is near the Outer Banks, North Carolina, and this project does not have much support up there." Explained Alexis. "That will weigh heavily—especially at the state level.   The two states have a very close relationship, and permitting something in South Carolina that will significantly and materially impact North Carolina doesn't happen unless both states agree."

"This is all well and good if I needed an analysis of Southern hospitality, but what I actually need is the legal argument for obtaining those permits." Replied Steve, the agitation in his voice reverberating through the conference room.

If Garett was phased, he did not let on. "It's all in there Steve, but you're going to need more than a legal argument on your side. Has North Carolina issued your client any advisory opinions on this matter?" He offered Steve some cream and sugar.

Steve emptied two single-use cream containers into his coffee and followed them up with a heaping teaspoon of sugar. "No, they've been completely silent on the matter, even before CTG withdrew the permit application up there. I understand there was quite a mob on the beach for weeks prior." With that he took a sip of his coffee and almost smiled. "Ahhh...good coffee." His lips smacked together.

Alexis took a long, savoring sip, breathed in the aroma, and imagined she was sitting in a blue-tiled coffee shop somewhere in Turkey. She turned her attention back to Steve and noticed a pigeon pecking at the exterior window sill behind his head.

"We're here to support you however we can, Steve. But it's going to be slow. And it will not be easy." Volunteered Garett.

"That's why I thought I'd come down here for a while to expedite things," responded Steve with a voice of confidence. "You wouldn't mind if I snagged an empty office for some weeks, would you Garett?" Steve failed to mention that he was in the midst of a divorce and needed a break from New Jersey.

"No, not at all," responded Garett, pokerfaced. This project was sounding bigger and longer to him than he ever imagined. Garett calculated in his mind how many billable hours he thought he could appropriate to his firm for Alexis' contribution. "Take all the time you need. We have an empty office available for you on the same floor as Alexis."

"Great; thank you, Garett." Steve said, now in a good mood. "Let me look at this memo and we can talk once I've had a chance to get through it."

Chapter 7: The Coffee Shortage

Marie sat at the bar at Two Hearts Coffee. She had gotten into the habit of coming in a couple of times a week. Brigg pulled up a seat next to her. "I've got a few minutes; Tom is filling in for me. How's it going?" He asked her.

"Pretty well. This place is starting to feel like home base to me. How are you doing?" She spun around to face him.

"Good. I've been thinking a lot about your project; the offshore drilling thing. It would be quite awful if it went through. There must be some huge interests you're going up against." He said, fiddling with her emptied sugar packet.

"I imagine there are. I'm glad I can't see them directly; otherwise it might be too overwhelming." She gave him a laugh to dismiss the thought and changed topics. "I talked to Sydney about the whale photos."

"Yeah? How did that go?" He asked with interest.

"Very well. What he had to say was really moving. He agreed to speak at a Surfers of the Sea reception for the ocean planning process next month. Actually, I was wondering: would you be interested in hosting it here at the coffee shop?" She asked.

Brigg thought about it for a second. "I am definitely interested." He looked around the room and noticed a line was starting to form at the register. "How about dinner at my place next week? We can talk over the details." He had already gotten up and was making his way toward the counter.

***

Later that week, Marie arrived at Brigg's house and knocked on the door. It was a modest two-story home just north of downtown.

"Hey, good to see you!" Brigg gave Marie a warm hug.

She was carrying a bottle of wine and a bag of pistachios. "Good to see you too!" She hugged him in return, careful not to let the bottle land on the back of Brigg's ribcage. The pistachios pressed against his left kidney. "I brought some things to go with dinner."

"Oh, great! I was just starting." He led her into the kitchen, where some chicken lay unwrapped from its butcher paper next to peppers and a bag of tortillas.

"That looks like a great foundation." Marie opened the bag of pistachios and poured them into a bowl. "Sorry—I'm super hungry, so I'm going to dig right in to these."

Brigg joined her. They stood there shelling pistachios and popping them into their mouths. "These are very satisfying somehow." Brigg commented.

"I know." Agreed Marie in between pistachios. "I love nuts." That sounded strange to her as it came out of her mouth, and her face became slightly flushed.

Brigg didn't seem to notice and instead turned to the wine Marie brought. "Would you be terribly offended if I added a little bit of this wine to the chicken? I imagine it would really go with this dish."

"Sounds delicious to me. I'm only going to have one glass of it at most, anyway. Do you want any help?"

"Sure, do you want to cut the peppers?" He retrieved a cutting board and knife. "How long have you been with Surfers of the Sea?" He then asked.

"Just a few years. I worked for ATF before." She said, accepting the peppers with two hands.

Brigg went over to the stove and began searing the chicken. "ATF? Is that Alcohol, Tobacco, Firearms?"

Marie nodded while chopping. "I was a special agent for them on the West Coast. Did a lot of criminal investigations."

"You mean you carried a gun?" Brigg asked with surprise.

"I did. And I had to stay super fit all the time. You never knew when you'd be asked to leap out of a building or do backflips for that job." Marie responded.

Brigg let out a laugh. "I see. You must have seen some crazy shit, then."

"Too much of it. At some point I was tired of it and needed to leave. I wanted to be in nature after that." She replied.

"How did you get into this line of work? Environmental activism, I mean?" Brigg asked.

She thought about where to start. "Well, in the beginning I was clueless about the environment, like many people. Then I began surfing and paying attention to the water. Then I became aware of how fragile marine life can be."

"And you started hanging out with Surfers of the Sea after that?" He prodded, slightly distracted by the stove.

"I met a few surfers who were part of SOS. Then I started doing some projects for them here and there. Well, it turned out I was pretty good at working on coastal conservation. So I stuck around." Marie brought the cutting board over to the stove.

"Do you ever miss it? The action and adventure of being an ATF agent?" Brigg asked her.

"Admittedly, I do. There was a certain excitement in arresting a criminal or preventing an illegal deal from happening." She looked at him almost apologetically. Then she changed the subject. "How about you? How did you end up owning a coffee shop?"

Brigg added the peppers into the pan and began sautéing them together with the chicken. "Well, I finished college with a biology degree and went off to study crocodiles in the Florida Everglades."

"I had no idea you did environmental work!" Marie exclaimed.

"Yeah; for a time." Brigg replied. "It was gut wrenching work, though. The crocodile habitat is being destroyed by development. And what's left is subject to industrial pollution. We saw a lot of evidence of hormone disrupting chemicals in their environment. I even saw baby crocodile hatchlings born with two heads."

Marie sucked in a breath of air. "That is horrible, Brigg!" She searched his eyes and then asked, "What are hormone disruptors, from a biologist's perspective? I've heard that term thrown around, but my understanding of what it means is pretty vague."

"They're man-made chemicals that interfere with the proper functioning of our bodies. They can interfere with growth and development—like with the crocodile hatchlings. Or they can interfere with our body's ability to do what it is designed to do on a daily basis—like maintain our body temperature, digest our food, and generate energy." Brigg took a break from the sauce pan.

"That sounds really broad. And potentially subtle at the same time. I mean, it's one thing to be born with an obvious birth defect, but another to feel off—like you're too hot or too cold. Or feel low on energy. Are these chemicals pretty rare or are they common?" Asked Marie.

"Unfortunately many birth defects are not obvious at all. People have slight changes in their organs and body physiology due to environmental pollution and don't even know it—these defects usually lead to health issues because their bodies are not as robust as they should be. And hormone disruptors are quite common. Actually, they're frequently produced from petroleum and then used to make products such as plastics, synthetic fragrances, and pesticides." Brigg lamented.

"Wait, these are produced from petroleum?" Asked Marie, straightening her spine. "You're telling me hormone disrupting chemicals are produced from petroleum and used to make stuff like plastics and fragrance? I mean, I knew waste from petroleum refining was used to make plastics, but I didn't realize it was so toxic…"

"Yeah. Unfortunately. A number of prominent ingredients in these types of products are hormone disruptors." Brigg nodded.

"Are they toxic when in the product? Or is it just the industrial waste that's the problem?" Marie pressed him for more information.

"Both. They're toxic when dumped as waste and toxic in the products when we consume them." He said, feeling slightly elated that someone was expressing interest in something related to his former research.

"This is huge!" Exclaimed Marie. "Brigg, we need to figure out how to get you to talk about this to a broader audience. I mean, this totally relates to our Oil Free Oceans Campaign. And the ocean planning process. Would you do that?"

"I guess so. I could talk a little bit about our research, but maybe you'd want to find someone more qualified to talk about hormone disruptors in consumer products and human health. Our research just focused on crocodiles."

Marie thought about this. "That makes sense. Let me look into it. I'd love to include your work as well, though. I think what's going on in the animal kingdom is really important."

"I agree." Brigg said enthusiastically. "What happens to animals is frequently an indicator of what ultimately happens to us."

"It sounds like you are really into this, Brigg. Why didn't you stick with the biology work?" Marie gave him a long look.

Brigg took five tortillas out of their bag. "I felt helpless to do anything about what I saw. Neither the EPA nor industry did anything in response to our findings. It was as if the problem didn't exist, as far as they were concerned. There were a few people who cared, but none of them could bring it to the attention of their managers…. "

"I'm sorry, Brigg. I know how that can be." She placed her hand closer to his.

"Thanks." He took a deep breath and looked at her with appreciation. "When my dad died, I came up to Charleston to help close up his affairs. The opportunity to buy this coffee shop came up and my brother and I took it. Our inheritance enabled us to do it and coffee was already a side-passion for both of us. That was three years ago. I haven't looked back."

"You still have a passion for the environment, though; I can see that." Observed Marie.

Brigg leaned back against the counter. "I haven't done much about it, though." He then grinned at her, "It's good that you're here. Maybe you can pull me back in."

***

Some days later, Marie wandered into the coffee aisle at Publix Supermarket. She had recently moved into a house nearby that she was sharing with a woman named Betsy. She liked that Betsy was quiet and tidy. The house itself was nothing special, although it was in close proximity to the architectural splendor of downtown. Marie was really beginning to settle in to her new life in Charleston, and even felt excited to be grocery shopping.

What caught her attention at that moment was the emptiness of the coffee shelves. There were a few bags of store-brand ground up beans, but nothing else. Someone had posted a laminated sign on the shelves that said, "Two bags maximum per customer." It was the only explanation. Marie decided to skip the generic coffee and go to Two Hearts the following day.

***

Marie biked over to Two Hearts the next morning. She took her time, exploring the smaller streets that ultimately led to Charleston Harbor and the French Quarter. She knew that most of Charleston did not look this way; it was like any other

American city with its fair share of parking lots, strip malls, and drive-through fast food restaurants. Nevertheless, she enjoyed immersing herself in this quaint urban landscape.

It was a Saturday and the cafe was full. Brigg was there with a long line of people waiting for their coffee. She found an empty seat and pulled out a book she had recently borrowed from the library: *The Soul of an Octopus*. She figured it would be best to read for a while until the line died down.

She was ten pages into the book when Brigg came up to her. "Hey!" He greeted Marie with her favorite latte. "It's been pretty crazy over here. A lot of people are complaining that the store shelves are out of coffee and are showing up on our doorstep. We've been busy all morning. How are you?"

"Pretty good; I just moved into my new place. I was at the grocery store yesterday too and the coffee was pretty much all out. I had the same idea as everyone else, and here I am." Marie put down her book and held the latte in two hands to enjoy its aroma. "Thank you so much, for this!"

"You're welcome." Brigg then changed the topic, "That looks like a good book. Anything interesting in there so far?"

"It says that fish have personalities; as do lobsters and sea anemones." Marie replied.

"I could tell you that from studying crocodiles. When they're resting, they can appear frozen in stone. For someone who is just passing by and taking pictures of them as a tourist, it may seem like there is not much more to them. But if you spend enough time with them, you will start to see the emotion in their eyes. And you definitely get a glimpse of their personalities when they're active. Most people miss all of that."

"I've never been close to crocodiles, but I would like to experience that sometime." Marie looked at Brigg with amazement.

 "That reminds me: I think I know of someone who you might want to contact as a potential speaker on hormone disruptors. Her name is Lorie Rubin and she used to be at the EPA. Now she works at Demson University." Brigg volunteered.

"That's awesome, Brigg; thank you! I'll reach out to her." Marie smiled at Brigg.

"Great!" He smiled back at her and then looked up abruptly to see more customers flowing in. "I've got to go over to the City Market in a little while to pick up some emergency supplies. This crowd has pillaged my pastries. Do you have time to join me? I need another half an hour or so here, and then my brother can take over."

"I'm in." Marie replied.

***

They walked past musicians playing trumpets, hat shops and clothing stores, the smell of shrimp sizzling, and the aroma of fresh-cut flowers. Everywhere they went there were overhead ceiling fans—a signature in Charleston. The breeze blew in through the open market halls. And the crowd seemed to be milling endlessly in circles looking at pottery, paintings, and soaps.

A few times Brigg held her hand so they would not get separated by the tourists. He finally stopped at a pastry shop and handed a sample to Marie. Bourbon, chocolate, and pecan clusters—they were delicious. He went on to pick up an assortment of cookies and pastries to take back to the cafe.

They discussed where to go next. The Gullah art gallery had caught her eye, with colorful paintings of people, flowers, and animals along the coast. They back-tracked their way, stopping between the open-air halls to admire enormous sweetgrass baskets and listen to the vendors talk Charleston history with the tourists.

"Who is that?" Asked Marie, as they saw a tall, dark African American woman being interviewed by the press near the Gullah art gallery. She was wearing a beautiful long dress and had sea shells in her hair. An overweight guy with a giant camera covering his entire chest was filming her giving a speech.

"I believe that is the Chieftess of the Gullah Gechee Nation. The original African ethnic groups who came over to the US as slaves. The Gulla Gechee are active in environmental justice and work to preserve the coastline. Just up your alley. Their environmental branch is known as the Gullah Gechee Sea Island Coalition." Brigg explained.

"Wow. She's impressive. I'll have to look up the Gullah Gechee Sea Island Coalition." She repeated the name to help her remember it.

They moved away quietly and began looking at the Gullah art gallery offerings. "How's it going with the ocean planning?" Brigg asked her as they looked through framed prints, which had been sorted neatly into wooden bins.

"Really good! I'm learning a lot about the region still. Oh! I've been meaning to ask you. What are you doing next Saturday? SOS is holding an Oil Free Oceans event at Savage Beach Resort. Roman Ferrari—the tennis player—will be there."

"Sounds like I am coming with you." He replied. "I'll invite my brother, too. He loves Roman Ferrari."

Chapter 8: Roman Ferrari

It was a cool, sunny day on Savage Beach one week later when SOS hosted its Oil Free Oceans beach party in Charleston, South Carolina. Roman Ferrari talked about the consequences of allowing offshore drilling and the importance of protecting the coast. There were two local news media sources filming the event. Roman was suave, vibrant, enthusiastic, and very charismatic. The large audience cheered and clapped.

A handful of small business owners in the area came up to Marie after Roman's speech, offering their support for SOS' Oil Free Oceans campaign. They included owners of a local fishing shop, a yoga studio, a restaurant, a walking tour company and a surf shop. A few of them volunteered to attend the South Atlantic planning workshops; others agreed to write letters to their state representatives. The surf shop offered to sponsor future SOS events related to offshore drilling. Marie felt the event was turning out to be a big success.

A couple of hours later, the crowd had finished eating a selection of sliders, slaw, and sweet potato fries. Some were still drinking beer or water. A few had brought wetsuits and were wriggling themselves into them, regarding the waves. Marie, Brigg, his brother Tom, Roman Ferrari and a half dozen others were clustered around the SOS tent. Brigg was telling them how he had not been able to secure a shipment of coffee anywhere for his coffee shop. He managed to scrounge up some beans from various places, but he anticipated that as of the middle of next week they would run dry.

"Oh my God!" One woman exclaimed in apocalyptic overtones. "What if the world is running out of coffee?"

"I tried a few coffee shops this morning on the way here and they were already out. Even Bert's Market up the street didn't have anything." Noted a guy in his early forties wearing a puffy vest.

"The Savage Beach Resort has already run out of coffee too," volunteered Roman. "Which reminds me, I need to go talk to the resort manager." He then excused himself from the group.

"What are you going to do if you run out of coffee, Brigg?" Asked Marie.

"We'll be serving tea—we've been talking to the Charleston Tea Company to feature their teas in our new menu. Tom and I are also thinking about coming up with a coffee substitute. We're planning to work on it this weekend."

"I pulled some herbalism books from the library for recipe ideas. There's lots of info in there about roasting roots and mixing herbs together for a pick-me up effect." Tom volunteered.

"We have to be careful, though." Brigg said, flexing his hands with slight hesitation. "Some herbs can have profound effects on people. I mean it's okay if whatever we create is slightly stimulating, but a lot of herbs should not be consumed for prolonged periods of time—we could end up causing people serious health problems. We don't want our product to be associated with giving people heart palpitations, for example."

"But doesn't coffee already give people heart palpitations?" Asked Tom.

"That's beside the point," replied Brigg. "We're going to be held to a different standard because we're creating something new; something of our own."

Marie, Brigg and a few of the Charleston Chapter volunteers began to dismantle the tables and canopy. "When I have a serious crisis or craving and can't have coffee, I make myself a Hot Mess." Marie told Brigg.

"What's a Hot Mess?" He asked with curiosity.

"It's dark chocolate mixed with hazelnut butter and rum soaked raisins. It tastes just like a hot mess. You could serve it in an espresso cup. That's probably just the right portion size. Any more and your customers would pass out."

"Will you teach me how to make it?"

"Yeah, definitely! How about Monday right after you close?"

"You're on." Brigg said his goodbye and Marie turned back to the task of dismantling the main tent.

Minutes later, she was aware that Brigg was running back in her direction from the parking lot. "Marie! Some guys just shoved Roman Ferrari into a van and took off. Tom's calling the police."

"What?" Marie stepped toward Brigg.

"We couldn't stop them; we were too far away and he was just about to get in his car. They picked him up like they'd been waiting for him." Brigg sounded deeply apologetic.

Marie's head spun at the thought that at her first Charleston event she had lost Roman Ferrari. She was almost confused about why she was there—to rally for the ocean or protect the celebrity tennis player as a former federal agent. She regained her sense of reality; the truth—in her perspective—lay somewhere in between. "Did you get a license plate?" She asked, assuming her former ATF role.

"Only part of it, unfortunately. Not enough to go by." Brigg was visibly distressed. "And they were in a white van."

Marie and Brigg jogged back over to the parking lot. "Which way did they go?" She asked as they reached visual distance of the street.

"Right around that corner. They could have gone anywhere." He observed.

"What did these guys look like? You said they were wearing masks?" Marie asked.

"Yeah; bank robber outfits. Black clothes, ski masks. They were big guys—looked quite fit; like they spend a lot of time working out. Two grabbed Roman, put a hood over his head and pulled him into the van. There was a third guy in the driver's seat. They peeled away right after." Brigg explained.

"Did they say anything? Did he say anything?" She prodded.

"No; they just pulled him in like they had rehearsed it ahead of time. Maybe they muffled him, I'm not sure." Brigg reflected back.

Tom got off the phone with the police and came over to meet them. "They said they'd be over to take our statements." He looked ashen.

"It sounds like these guys had some experience with this sort of thing. And it definitely sounds like a kidnapping. I'm gonna go out on a limb here and have you guys call the press. The sooner this gets in the news the better chance we may have of finding him quickly. Can you do that for me while I go talk with the resort manager?" Marie was already backing up toward the beach.

She ran through the parking lot, landscaped gardens, and into the main building. The manager, a slim blond woman in her thirties, invited Marie to her office.

"Did he come speak to you before he left?" Marie asked walking into the room, remembering that Roman planned to do so.

"Yes; he was here." The manager took a seat at her office chair, and Marie sat down across from her. "Julia Lockhart," she introduced herself to Marie.

"Marie Alpern. I'm with Surfers of the Sea. I'm also a former federal agent—so I am feeling responsible for not being able to prevent this." Marie's face fell. She seemed to shake off the feeling and took a quick look around the office, including Julia's pictures of her dogs.

"I'm so sorry." Julia took a deep breath. "First the coffee mold and now this."

"You mean the coffee shortage?" Marie asked, feeling confused.

"Not exactly. Before any of that we had an incident. The coffee from our supplier was completely moldy and made the guests sick. It was during the time that Roman was playing in a tournament. I called the supplier and they sent us a fresh batch, but they would not admit to any wrong doing." Julia played with her necklace absentmindedly, an uncomfortable look on her face.

"Is it possible that there was some sort of an intentional contamination? I mean, to target Roman somehow?" Marie blinked, staring at the photos of the dogs again.

Julia opened her palms toward the ceiling fan. "Could be. I just assumed it was something on the supplier's end—at the time." She then shifted gears. "You said you worked as a federal agent?"

"Yes; for ATF. Alcohol, tobacco, firearms, and explosives. I mostly investigated drug-related violent crimes." Marie explained.

"I hope we won't need your skillset now." Julia commented, studying Marie as if trying to decide whether the woman in front of her had the physical capacity to arrest anyone.

"Did he say where he was going after Charleston?" Marie ignored Julia's comment.

The manager thought for a while. "Roman was flying back to Italy. He said he was about to do some sort of coffee promotion for his sponsor."

"Which sponsor?" Marie asked.

Julia rubbed at her cheek. "Luca. They make high-end espresso machines."

"Do you have a contact phone number or email for someone at Luca? I should call them. And ask if Roman had any enemies or whether there has been any other trouble recently." Marie was thinking ahead.

Julia turned to her computer. "Hold on. Let me look them up. Do you have an email address where I can send this to you?"

She pulled out a pair of glasses from her desk drawer and put them on before searching her computer screen.

Marie took her card out from her purse and gave it to Julia. "Did anything else unusual happen during Roman's stay? Any strange people hanging about?" She felt hurried to get as much information as possible.

Julia leaned back into her chair again, taking off her glasses. "No, nothing unusual that I can remember."

"Will you call me if you remember anything else?" Marie insisted, leaning her palms into the elbow rest.

"I will." Julia got up with Marie and saw her to the door.

By the time the police arrived, the rest of the SOS party had packed up their gear and stood or sat on the parking lot curb. The local TV channels had arrived. It appeared they had sent the same anchor people who attended the Oil Free Oceans event.

Brigg and Tom were talking to the police. When they saw Marie, they waived her over.

"You're the former ATF agent?" Asked an older police officer.

"Yes; now I'm with Surfers of the Sea. We co-hosted an event here with the Savage Beach Resort. I just spoke to their manager, Julia Lockhart."

"Both of you will need to speak with the FBI." The police officer realized this case would be out of his hands soon.

"Okay." Marie answered. "But you should know that Roman Ferrari was sponsored by a high end espresso machine maker and that the coffee at this resort was tainted during Roman's stay. The club manager can tell you more about that."

Chapter 9: The Mold Crisis

Announcer: "Cities around the country are experiencing coffee supply disruptions due to a severe outbreak of a new strain of toxic mold. The mold has quickly spread through coffee shipping containers, distributor's warehouses, and roasting facilities.

The mold issue was first identified at the Savage Beach Resort in Charleston, South Carolina. It poisoned guests during the resort's annual international tennis tournament. Italian tennis star Roman Ferrari, who is also the brand ambassador for Luca espresso machines, was playing at the resort at the time and was kidnapped soon after. No word has been received regarding Roman's whereabouts. The FBI is now looking into the connection between Ferrari's disappearance and the coffee mold.

All beans infected with the mold are being destroyed per government mandate to stop the spread of the disease. Consumers are advised not to purchase coffee beans produced after May 15th of this year, as tainted coffee is known to cause severe nausea, headaches, diarrhea, and vomiting. Border authorities have also issued a moratorium on any import or export of coffee to contain this serious outbreak."

"Chris, did you hear that?" Tucker exclaimed, nearly bumping his head on the hood of the car he was working on.

"What?" Yelled Chris from the other side of the screen door.

"The coffee mold! It's taken over!" Tucker was bursting with shock and excitement.

Chris pushed the screen door open with his foot and emerged into the garage holding two beers. "What coffee mold?"

What do you mean, "What coffee mold?" Responded Tucker, waiving a wrench in one hand. "The shit you spread at the Savage Beach? It's taken over the country!"

"What?" Asked Chris, laughing in disbelief.

"Dude! It's all over the radio! Your coffee mold's shut down the entire coffee supply." Tucker was getting quite excited.

"No way, man!" Chris replied. "That couldn't really happen! Could it?"

"Well, it just did! Where's my cell phone? We've got to Google this. You just trashed the entire coffee supply in the US, man! People are going to be pissed!"

***

Chris visited Jamie's parents' house the following week, when he knew Jamie would be there, to deliver the bad news.

"It's you! Have you come to pay my money back?" Jamie asked opening the door, barely bothering to lower his voice for his parent's sake.

Chris waived him onto the porch; he apparently wanted to talk in private. "Look, bud. I snagged a sample of your science project from the lab when I came to visit you, and I dumped it on the coffee beans at the resort at work. That shit spread like wildfire!"

Chris was in a mild panic.

Jamie looked down at Chris like a jogger might look down at a small barking dog. "Chris. You don't spread plant diseases by dumping mold on roasted coffee. That's absurd! You pay me back that money or I will get it from your dad. And stay away from the lab!" He turned away to go back inside.

"Nah, Jamie, I'm telling you! They were all sick! The guests and everything!" Chris stepped toward Jamie.

Jamie turned back around and pinched the bridge of his nose with his hand. "Chris, I don't know exactly what you did or why, and I don't really want to know. If you serve people moldy coffee they will probably get sick. That has little to do with the current coffee crisis, which obviously began at the farm. When I say the farm, I'm not talking about the farm in South Carolina because we don't grow coffee beans here. I'm talking about places like South America and Africa, where actual coffee plants grow. That's where mold matters. Just consider yourself lucky that you didn't kill anyone." Jamie gave Chris the most condescending look he could muster and then walked back into the house and slammed the screen door behind him.

***

"Angelo, thanks so much for meeting with me," said Francesco as he shook the hands with the CEO of Luca USA. Both men sat down and regarded each other with anticipation.

"Thanks for coming, Francesco. I know this has been a difficult time for all of us," stated Angelo. He fiddled with the wedding band around his finger. "I know Roman is a personal friend of yours."

"I've known him for years." Francesco looked very tired. "Has there been a ransom note?"

"No; nothing yet." Angelo replied. "The FBI is looking into it. I've not been able to speak to anyone in charge. They're happy, however, to take messages from 'parties with any relevant information.' I did ask them to have the investigating agent give me a call."

"That doesn't sound very encouraging." Francesco held his fist to his mouth. "Poor Roman. He's got to be alive; there must be some reason they took him. It sounds like there's some connection between his kidnapping and the coffee mold."

"There is a woman there in Charleston—an environmental activist who knows Roman and was there when he was kidnapped. She's a former federal agent and spent seven years investigating drug-related crimes. I think we should hire her for Roman's sake." Angelo stated, looking at Francesco thoughtfully.

"She didn't prevent Roman from getting kidnapped." Francesco commented icily. Then he spread his fingers on the desk and sighed. "Maybe she feels responsible."

"Maybe. We're likely to get a lot more information from hiring her than by relying on the FBI, alone, I'm pretty sure." Urged Angelo.

"Okay. Hire her." Francesco agreed. He shifted his weight from his right hip to his left. "And what about the coffee mold situation?"

"It's unlikely to change any time soon," replied Angelo. "Our sales are suffering because we're lacking the very thing our product relies upon. We need to come up with our own solution, because the situation is unlikely to take care of itself."

"I understand your point of view Angelo. What do you propose?"

Angelo took a deep breath. "I propose that we come out with a premium coffee substitute exclusively for our customers."

Francesco leaned back in his chair and clasped his hands behind the back of his head. He thought of how a number of large companies had built empires selling substitute products during wartime. What came first and foremost to mind was Nescafe.

"I can support this Angelo, but we have to come up with something unique; something that has a notable positive impact on the taste buds of our customers. We Italians are no strangers to herbal concoctions. Maybe we could utilize some of that traditional knowledge to put something together. Should I call the home office about this?"

"I think we need to find a beverage designer within the United States." Replied Angelo.

"Do you have some leads, Angelo?" Francesco asked.

Angelo leaned in. "I have a close friend at a specialty roaster in Portland, Oregon. Her company has a top notch reputation and I hear there's already a race to create a viable coffee substitute over there. We need to get in there and be the first to get our product out to a national market."

"Does she know how to do dark roast well, Angelo? I hear the Portland market is flooded with these lighter roast coffees. I wouldn't want our reputation to be tainted by them." Francesco bit his lip.

"Of course not. Who in their right mind wants their coffee to taste like a grapefruit or a tomato? They can drink juice if they want a grapefruit. No, no; this roaster knows how to make coffee; she's Italian. " Angelo sat back in his seat confidently.

"Molto bene, Angelo; I'll give you the go-ahead. But I need results in the next few days, as we have to make some decisions."

***

The following Monday afternoon Marie knocked on the front door at Two Heart's Coffee. Brigg was inside setting mixing bowls on the main counter. "Nice to see you Marie," He gave her an enveloping hug once he opened the door.

"Nice to see you too, Brigg! It feels like ages since I saw you last, even though it was only a couple of days." Marie returned the hug and pecked Brigg on the cheek. "I've had a rough day and I'm ready for some chocolate."

"I'm so sorry about Roman." Brigg said to her. He had the urge to kiss Marie's lips, but decided against following through.

"I feel responsible, although there is no reason I should feel that way. " She admitted, taking her jacket off.

"Well, hopefully some of this will make you feel better." Brigg pulled out a large block of chocolate, a jar of hazelnut butter, and a glass container with rum-soaked raisins.

"Thanks." She reached for the chocolate. "You know how Roman Ferrari was sponsored by that espresso machine company?"

"Yes—Luca, right?" Brigg was rummaging around for more supplies.

"They want to hire me to find Roman." She said, opening the jar of hazelnut butter.

"What did you tell them?" Brigg asked, feeling suddenly protective of Marie.

"I told them I would do the best I can." She answered.

"Are you going to be sneaking around breaking into buildings?" Asked Brigg skeptically.

"I hope not. I don't have any back-up team to do that sort of thing. But I can ask around and help the FBI agent." She replied.

"Be careful, Marie." Brigg looked at her with concern.

"You're worried about me?" She asked.

"Yes." He folded his arms.

"Thank you." She replied, genuinely touched.

Half an hour later, they were tasting what they had made. "This stuff is like a kick in the pants, Marie. I don't even know how I'm going to get to sleep tonight." Brigg said, reaching for another nibble.

Marie pushed his arm away. "Well, you can start by leaving some for the customers."

"Okay, okay." He covered the fragrant mixture and started to clean up.

"Oh; there's this other delicious thing I used to make! Its an affogato with cream porter beer, vanilla ice cream, and coffee… but we don't have the coffee, though." She frowned as the realization hit home again.

"I've had beer and ice cream floats with coffee before; their delicious." Said Brigg. A moment later his eyes lit up. "I have some freeze dried coffee a friend of mine gave me as a joke when we opened up the cafe." He went into the back room and started to rummage around in a corner cabinet. He returned a few moments later, with a 64 ounce container of Nescafe Gold Dark Roast.

Marie stared at the Nescafe container feeling doubtful. "Are you sure it's still good? It sounds like it's been sitting around back there for three years."

"I've never opened it and it's Nescafe. It's designed to withstand anything. The astronauts even took it to the moon." He set the container down, unscrewed the cap and gently pulled at the foil seal, peeling back the first inch of it.

Marie came closer and took a deep whiff. "Oh my god; this smells so good!"

Brigg covered the foil seal over the jar again and sealed the cap back on. "Sunday ice cream social with cream porter, vanilla ice cream and Nescafe. We could make it a special event for the SOS Oil Free Oceans campaign."

"That would be fabulous!" Exclaimed Marie. "I'd like to do it on the topic of hormone disruptors and their connection to offshore drilling. I corresponded with Lorie Rubin, the

researcher you mentioned at Demson University. She said sh'e
be thrilled to come out. I just need to secure my other speaker—
the one who'd talk about crocodiles." She looked at Brigg with
anticipation. "Will you do it, Brigg?"

"For you? Yes." He smiled and put his arms around Marie,
lifting her off the floor in the process.

Chapter 10: The PR Lady

Steve left his hotel room and walked to the office at Whyte, Farm & Bellingham. It was already 8:30 am, later than he had hoped to get in. He didn't sleep very well last night, his mind obsessing about the CTG project. Alexis had recommended in her memo that the legal team focus on lobbying the government agencies to secure CTG's interests in offshore drilling.

Steve cringed at the thought of bargaining with government agency employees, especially the planner types. His experience was that as a profession they were trained to deflect all controversial matters with silence or by stringing together vague and non-committal statements. He imagined it was a reflex borne by years of interfacing with the public, which was always pissed off about something. Steve was used to making straightforward arguments in a courtroom while going up against straightforward lawyers, without the evasive goo of bureaucrats or local politics. He felt he did not know how to talk to these people.

His worries had drifted into his dreams. Last night he dreamt that he was at the office of a construction company in

Charleston. The project manager was showing Steve a model of a crude oil storage terminal his client wanted to build nearby. A giant tidal wave approached outside and crashed through the glass walls of the building, washing away the model and sweeping Steve with it into Charleston Harbor.

In his dream, Garett suddenly appeared with his sailboat and asked whether Steve wanted a lift. Garett fished him out of the water and once Steve was safely dragged onto the hull, the Charleston attorney folded his arms and said, "I told you that you should have talked to those planners first—now everything's washed away."

Maybe Steve could personally attend the public meetings but leave it to Alexis to engage with the South Carolina agency people, since the law firm was local and had some connections already. That would still leave Steve free to focus on the legal issues at the federal level to secure a drilling permit for CTG.

He walked into Whyte, Farm & Bellingham feeling more assured about this distribution of tasks. He swung by Alexis' office. Her computer was on but she wasn't in the room. He wandered down the hall to the break room in search of coffee.

"Ah, here you both are!" He found Alexis and Garett in the break room.

"How is that hotel treating you? Did you sleep well?" Asked Alexis.

"Hotel's fine, thanks, but I didn't sleep very well." Responded Steve. "I'm troubled by some of the highlights in your recent memo, Alexis. I am not a fan of politics."

Alexis stood there, not sure what to say. She decided it would be best for Garett to answer, since he seemed to know Steve.

"Steve, you know as much as I do that even the law is influenced by politics. We just don't often get directly involved, that's all." Garrett lectured him.

***

Steve sat in his office later that morning. Garett and Alexis had just left after an extensive phone call with CTG. The company decided it would be best to send a strategist down to attend the regional ocean planning meetings with Steve. She would be the voice for the company; his role would be to sit and listen.

Steve knew the woman who was coming down. Chandra West. He met her working for other clients. Something must be up. He hadn't seen Chandra work on anything but cases where the client was in some sort of hot water.

The CEO of the company joined in on the call as well, which almost never happened. In the middle of the conversation, he brought up the kidnapping of a tennis player by the name of Roman Ferrari. "I thought he was supposed to be kidnapped by some environmentalists." The CEO had said, sounding both accusing and apologetic.

Chandra West had chimed in, calling the kidnapping a "PR disaster." What did that mean? And why bring up the topic at all? Both Steve and Chandra were billing at nearly $900 per hour. CTG wouldn't have talked about the kidnapping if it were not relevant somehow. What did Roman Ferrari have to do with offshore drilling?

Steve searched the Internet for news articles about the Roman Ferrari kidnapping. Most of them mentioned he had been kidnapped from the Savage Beach Resort and his endorsement of the Luca espresso brand.

Steve entered "Roman Ferrari" and "offshore drilling" together into the search browser. A series of articles popped up covering Roman Ferrari's speech at the Surfers of the Sea Oil Free Oceans event, which took place the same day as his kidnapping.

Neural cells started to fire in various parts of Steve's brain. Admittedly, Steve had a tendency toward paranoia, but sometimes his suspicions were justified. Could CTG have something to do with this kidnapping? Chandra couldn't have been involved, or else she wouldn't have admitted it was a PR disaster. Maybe she was being called in as the clean-up lady.

What if CTG had staged the kidnapping? And why would they do that? Would Kenny who had worked on this case before dropping dead of a heart attack have gotten wind of this? Did it contribute to his heart attack? Or did he really even have a heart attack? A strange tingling sensation poured over Steve's spine like hot syrup.

***

By Wednesday morning, Marie was at Two Heart's Coffee again. She had made little progress with respect to Roman Ferrari, although she had spoken to one of the FBI agents on the case the day before. He was making inquiries regarding Ferrari's activities in Charleston. Everyone was secretly waiting for the ransom note to arrive.

Marie turned her attention back to ocean planning when Brigg's brother, Tom, slipped into the seat across from her. "Marie," he whispered with almost a comical intensity.

"Yeah?" She peeled her eyes away from the computer screen.

"Don't look. There are two guys sitting behind you that just came in. A customer overheard them here a few weeks ago. They were joking about kidnapping Roman Ferrari and talking about slipping something into his coffee. And they said something about the Savage Beach Resort." Tom looked green around the gills.

"Are you serious?" Asked Marie in a low voice.

"Yes. Very serious." He whispered.

Marie sat there for a moment, thinking. "Okay. Here's what I want you to do. Go back to the bar and take some photos of these guys with your phone. Be as discreet as possible. When you're done, signal me by bringing me a cup of water. Then I'll go talk to them. And text the photos to the FBI agent. You've got his number?"

Tom nodded. "Okay," his voice was barely a whisper. He got up and left slowly.

Marie could see the reflection of one of the guys behind her in her computer screen. He was leaning back in his chair. She tried to focus on what he was saying.

"Jamie's been calling me a lot the last few days—he wants his money." Came the voice from behind her.

"You'd better pay him." It was the voice of the other guy. "Otherwise he might tell the police about your coffee mold."

"It's not my coffee mold! It's Jamie's."

Tom appeared and set a cup of water next to Marie. "Thank you," she said calmly, and took a sip. She then picked up her chair and carried it over to the guys sitting behind her.

"Mind if I join you guys?" She asked, setting her chair down without waiting for an answer.

They stared at her without responding. One of them maybe thought she was trying to hit him up for a date. She decided to take that angle.

"What are your names?" She asked with half-hearted flirtatiousness.

"I'm Tucker," said the guy who she thought had some romantic interests. "And this is Chris." Chris just sat there with his arms folded.

"Tucker, Chris—nice to meet you. I'm Marie. I'm investigating Roman Ferrari's disappearance. A customer overheard you in the cafe a few weeks ago joking about kidnapping him and slipping something into his coffee."

"Are you serious?" It was Chris, letting out a laugh of disbelief. "Roman's disappearance?"

"It was in the news…I forgot to tell you. Along with that coffee mold story." Tucker looked at Chris, somewhat distressed.

"You look concerned, Tucker. Is there anything the matter?" Asked Marie.

"No; no, not at all," Tucker replied unconvincingly. He was visibly shaken.

"Well, then why were you guys talking about the Savage Beach Resort? That's where Roman was last seen. And where the coffee mold problem started."

"Oh, nah…nah…that's not possible. Jamie told me that mold couldn't have spread to the rest of the country. It had to have developed at the coffee plantations." It was Chris this time who got up in arms.

"What mold?" Asked Marie. "You mean the coffee mold that you spread around the Savage Beach Resort?"

Chris backed his torso into his chair. "Nah…that was tobacco mold from over at Demson. That was no coffee mold. It was just a little joke."

"Demson?" Asked Marie, the name not ringing a bell.

"Chris' cousin works over at Demson University in a research lab. He does research on tobacco mold." Tucker volunteered.

"Would that be Jamie?" Marie asked, wanting to get as much information out of them as possible while they were still talking.

"I stole some of his mold when he was not looking. I told him about it later but he told me the mold couldn't have spread like that." Chris seemed genuinely flustered.

"Do either of you own a white unmarked van?" She asked, trying to return back to the topic of Roman.

Tucker stared at Chris strangely. "I do; Chris borrows it on occasion."

Chris started laughing again in disbelief. "Wha…you guys think
I snubbed off Roman Ferrari? How do you know he's not on
vacation or something? Maybe he just got tired and skipped
town?"

"Because witnesses saw him being kidnapped by three guys in a
white unmarked van. They were wearing ski masks at the time."
Marie stared at Chris, her arms folded. Chris seemed genuinely
unaware about the circumstances of Ferrari's disappearance.
She decided to try another angle. "Maybe you and Tucker here
and your cousin Jamie decided to kidnap Ferrari because you
didn't like him for some reason. Maybe he was inconvenient to
you? Found out about the mold problem?"

"What? No! What is this? Who are you, anyway?" Asked
Chris, getting red.

"Former ATF." Responded Marie, keeping her arms in place.
"And I've got a professional interest in finding Roman."

"What was your name again?" It was Tucker.

"Marie." She offered.

"Marie, I didn't kidnap Roman and I know Chris and his cousin Jamie certainly didn't." Tucker was gaining some confidence.

"How can you be so sure about that?" Asked Marie.

"Cause Jamie doesn't even like Chris—they're barely on speaking terms." Tucker exclaimed.

"Where did you say this Jamie works?"

***

The following afternoon Marie drove the distance to the Demson University Pee Dee Research Center. She had phoned ahead after Chris agreed to give her Jamie's contact info. She wanted to meet this Jamie for herself. And the FBI was now looking into Chris, Tucker, and Jamie's whereabouts at the time of the kidnapping.

Marie phoned Jamie from the parking lot when she got to the research campus. He came and greeter her at the front door.

"Thanks for seeing me." She smiled and offered her hand, which he took reluctantly.

Jamie led her through a series of narrow hallways into a break room. They sat down at a small table.

"I hear your cousin came to visit you here a few weeks ago?" She said it half as a question, half as a statement.

"Yes. He snuck in and came to see me in my lab space asking for money." Jamie's facial muscles flexed in various directions.

"And he stole some of the mold you were working on?" Marie looked at Jamie.

"That's what he told me later. He still hasn't returned the money, though." Jamie commented.

"Are you aware that he contaminated the coffee supply at Savage Beach Resort?" Marie asked him firmly.

"What? No, not really." He rubbed his face, and then changed his mind. "He might have said something like that to me but I wasn't really listening. I thought it was some poor excuse for not paying me."

He seemed uncomfortable, but not too concerned, thought Marie. "Did he say anything else to you at the time?"

"That he thought he'd contaminated the global coffee supply. I told him that was absurd," Jamie said impatiently and with some sense of sarcasm.

"Why is that?" Marie asked.

"Because you'd have to introduce the coffee mold at the coffee plantation—not spread it on roasted coffee beans. You can't contaminate the global coffee supply by letting mold grow in your coffee maker." He explained.

"Coffee mold?" Asked Marie. "I thought you were working on tobacco."

"That's the subject of my research. I've been breeding aggressive coffee mold with a non-aggressive variety and biologically modifying them for applications on tobacco plants. Our goal is to breed aggressive mold with non-aggressive mold so that the mold living on tobacco becomes non-aggressive and essentially harmless in subsequent generations." Jamie sounded very tired.

"What do you mean by 'biologically modifying' the mold?" Marie asked.

"Gene editing. You take the DNA from one strain of mold and put it into another." He explained, gesturing with his right hand like he was cutting with a pair of scissors.

"And are you sure that couldn't have somehow gotten out of control when your cousin stole a sample and contaminated the Savage Beach Resort's coffee?" Marie persisted.

"That would not be possible, as I have already told Chris. Those are roasted beans. He would have had to travel to Brazil or somewhere like that and contaminate the plants. But even that wouldn't have amounted to much, as I've been working on a strain that is meant for tobacco, not coffee." He folded his arms and leaned back.

Marie sat there in silence. The connection was still quite
uncanny. "Has anyone from your group travelled internationally
in the last month or so?" She finally asked.

"Just my boss; he went on vacation." Jamie responded.

"Is he here now?" Marie urged, thinking he would be worth
talking to.

"No; not today. He's got meetings off campus."

It had taken Marie two hours to drive up to Demson and she
would need another two hours to get back. At the same time, she
felt the pressure to go back to her Atlantic Ocean planning work.
She decided to tell the FBI agent about her conversation with
Jamie and recommend he look into the coffee mold situation and
Jamie's boss. Maybe a ransom note or other information would
come to light between now and then. She thanked Jamie for his
time and left the campus.

Chapter 11: Looking for Kidnappers

A few days later, Roman Ferrari had been found. The
kidnappers had left him tied up in a dumpster adjacent to a tire
repair shop located in a light industrial space. One of the
workmen found him yelling through duct tape he had half torn
off his mouth and banging against the side of the dumpster.
Marie heard about it on the radio just as she was driving back
from a meeting. The announcer said Roman was otherwise
unharmed, had been taken into police custody, and subsequently
released to the Savage Beach Resort to recover. Marie pulled
over and texted Julia Lockhart. "Thank God," came her reply.

Saturday morning she received a phone call from Roman
Ferrari, asking her to meet him at the Savage Beach Resort. She
got in her car and drove over. He sat on a beach chair facing the
ocean. He looked like he had been there for hours.

"I talked to Francesco at Luca. He told me you were a federal
agent," Roman said after she had taken a chair and sat down
next to him.

She had been practicing a formal apology to issue to him on behalf of Surfers of the Sea and didn't expect this. "Yes; I worked for ATF; the Bureau of Alcohol, Tobacco, Firearms and Explosives."

He looked at her directly for a long moment. "Shouldn't that be called ATFE?"

"Probably; but everyone calls it ATF. It just sounds better." She smiled at him, feeling awkward talking about the ambiguity of the ATF acronym to a kidnap victim.

"A special agent?" He asked.

"For seven years," She nodded, "before I started working with Surfers of the Sea." A long pause followed. "I'm sorry, Roman. I had no idea what was coming and if I had known, I would have done everything I could to prevent it from happening."

"That was the worst part. I was going about my day never expecting this. Then they pulled me off the street and there was nothing I could do about it. I'm a strong healthy guy and there was nothing I could do about it." He stared off into the ocean again, his hands resting flat on the arms of the beach chair. "My wife, on the other hand, she woke up Saturday morning with a terrible premonition. She didn't tell me at the time."

Marie sat next to him on the beach in silence. "Where is your wife now?" She finally asked.

"She's teaching a tennis workshop in the main court." He motioned vaguely behind him.

Marie thought about Roman's sense of helplessness. "Did they treat you decently?" She asked.

"They left me alone." He replied. "Not knowing how long I would be there or why was difficult for me." Then he let out a slight laugh. "Not shaving for days, not showering or combing my hair and wearing the same underwear; that was rough too."

"That's not exactly like camping; sounds much more uncomfortable." She volunteered.

"Especially when you are locked in a small room without windows. The air is not so fresh inside compared to the outdoors." He mused.

She imagined the stale air of a windowless room in contrast to the breeze off the shoreline they gazed upon.

"Marie," He leaned over closer to her. "I need you to find the kidnappers for me. The FBI are not doing much; they haven't even come around to interview me yet."

She chewed on her lip. "I'll do my best, Roman. I do need to cooperate with the FBI, though. And hopefully they will help me."

"They're coming to interview me on Thursday morning. Can you be there?"

"Yes; I think so."

Thank you." He breathed a sigh of relief and looked more confident. "What can I tell you?"

"How many of them were there?"

"Three that I know of."

"Any personal identifying features?"

He shook his head. "They kept their masks on the entire time."

"Did you have any sense of where you were going after they pulled you into the van?" She asked.

He sat there for a moment, his lips in a straight line. "I could tell we were weaving through the side streets and a few minutes later I was pretty sure we were going over a bridge. The road seemed fast-moving for a while, and then we veered off into another part of town. The van finally stopped, and the driver got out and I assumed he opened the garage. We drove in and parked. They closed the garage door before pulling me out of the vehicle. I had the sense we were in some sort of a warehouse."

"Did they say anything to you at all? About the coffee mold or why they kidnapped you?"

"They were silent until they pulled me into a side room. Then they took off the hood they had thrown over my head and told me I was going to be staying there for a while. I asked them why I was there and they never told me. Later on I started asking how long I would be there and if there was anything I could do to get released and they just told me to be patient." He chewed on his lip, remembering all of this.

"What did this room look like—where you stayed?" She asked

"Gray concrete walls and floor. It was possibly meant to be an office space, but there was no desk. There was a couch, a small refrigerator, and an adjacent bathroom."

"What did they feed you?" She asked.

"Mostly Thai food. And in the morning they would bring me donuts. There were also some snacks in the refrigerator."

"Was the food take-out?"

"Yes. The Thai food came in brown paper bags. As did the donuts."

"What kind of donuts?"

"There were some plain ones glazed with a sugar glaze. They were the size of small bagels. And some little round brown ones —I think they were supposed to be chocolate, but they didn't taste like chocolate to me. They were the size of golf balls."

"You mean donut holes?"

"Donut holes? I guess they looked like they came from the hole of the bigger donuts. Is that what you mean?" His Italian accent came through.

"I guess so." She tried to imagine how donuts are actually made. "Did they talk to you about anything while you were there?"

"No, they barely said a word to me. When they came in to give me food and to check up on me, they ignored all of my questions and told me to be patient."

"Did you see or hear anything that might offer any other insight about them or your location?"

He frowned in thought. "They kept me in that room and I couldn't hear much of what was going on in the rest of the space. And they wore their masks on when they came to visit me. But the day they let me out they had an argument, and I could hear a little bit of what they said. It sounded like two of the guys barged in and yelled to the third one who was guarding me that it was time to let me go. The guy guarding me asked what they meant and what happened to the plan? One of the other guys said the client won't pay for them any more and got cold feet." They swore a lot after that. Roman stopped talking and looked at Marie. "That was it." Then they tied me up, took me out of there and left me in a dumpster.

That wasn't much to go on, thought Marie. The client got cold feet, but there were no clues regarding who these guys were or who hired them. Donut holes and Thai food. Marie wondered whether anyone besides Dunkin' Donuts sold donut holes in the Charleston area. She would have to look into it.

"Where were you heading when they picked you up?" She asked

"I was going to my car to retrieve an extra pair of sunglasses."

"You weren't actually heading out anywhere?"

"No."

Marie showed Roman the pictures of Chris and Tucker that Tom had taken. "Do either of these guys look familiar to you?"

"No. Should they?" He replied after she flipped through the photos.

"I don't know. This one works at the Savage Beach Resort." Marie showed him a picture of Chris again.

Roman stared at it blankly. "I'm sorry. I've never noticed him."

"Hold on…let me find another picture." She searched for and found photo of Jamie on the Demson University website.

"No, I don't recognize him either." Roman said, almost apologetically.

"Will you and your wife be staying at the resort for a while?"

"We were supposed to fly out this upcoming Wednesday but we cancelled the flight, as we did not know what was happening with the FBI investigation. The resort invited us to stay as their guests."

***

Later that day, Marie sat down at her laptop and searched for Dunkin' Donuts in the Charleston area. There were a number of them. She would need to visit each one and see whether their staff remembered any guys coming in for several days in a row. Roman had been missing Saturday through Thursday, so she decided to do her Dunkin' Donuts tour on those days.

The next day was Tuesday, a perfect time to go. She went through her list and visited the first handful of Dunkin' Donuts in the morning with no luck. The staff people she talked to couldn't remember much. "So many people come in and there are a number of us working here," one employee apologized. She considered whether she could obtain security camera records from them; she'd need the FBI's help for that.

After Dunkin' Donuts #3, she decided to break for lunch. "Thai food near me," she searched on her phone. A reasonable looking place showed up within a couple of miles. Why not give it a try? She thought. Marie only wished Roman was there to join her — he might remember the flavor nuances in the food.

The restaurant was decorated tastefully, the walls painted a dark plum. Mirrors extended the light along the back and side walls. Beautifully woven tablecloths lay under slabs of glass, keeping them eternally clean. Marie ordered a noodle dish and watched the staff.

The food arrived and she ate thoughtfully. Somehow she knew she had to get on the same page as the FBI investigator for the case, but she anticipated that he would not be enthusiastic about cooperating with her, a private investigator. Marie didn't own a gun and she began musing how she would deal with Roman's kidnappers once she found them, especially if they did not wish to speak to her.

The matron of the restaurant came over. "How's the food?" She asked.

"It's great, thank you." Before the woman could walk away, Marie started her inquiry: "Did you by any chance have a strong-looking guy come by for take out Saturday through Thursday last week?

"Big guy, blond hair. He got an order for four on Saturday through Wednesday. Is he a friend of yours?" She was enthusiastic and friendly.

"Not exactly." Marie felt a rush of excitement at this piece of news. "Do you know Roman Ferrari, the tennis player? He was kidnapped last week Saturday. He's been released to safety but says he remembers eating Thai food." Marie tried to tell the story concisely.

The matron stepped back as if someone had accused her of the kidnapping crime. "We don't know anything about any kidnapping," she said.

"I can understand that; but it sure would help us to know the identity of the man who ordered the take-out from you." Marie explained. "Can you describe him to me?"

"He was a tall guy. Over six feet, you know? Short hair." She paused and thought about it some more. "I don't remember anything else about him."

"Did he give his name? You may have written it down on an order slip if he phoned in." Marie asked her.

"I don't remember a name. We don't keep order slips around; they went out with the trash. Let me talk to my husband. Hold on." She retreated and disappeared.

Marie was mostly done with her meal when the husband arrived. "May I help you?" He asked with a smile as if nothing had been relayed to him.

Marie repeated her story to him patiently. "Could you help us figure out who these guys were? Maybe you remember the name of the guy who came in?"

He scratched his head. "No; sorry."

"Do you remember anything else about him?" Marie asked. "What he looked like?"

"He was a tall, big guy. Muscular. I don't remember anything else." He was apologetic.

"What about credit card records? You probably have them unless he paid with cash. We could track him down that way." Marie suggested. "And there are probably phone records from when he called in as well."

"Where did you say you are from?" He asked her, feeling uncomfortable.

"I'm a former Bureau of Alcohol, Tobacco, Firearms and Explosive agent. I was hired by the victim to help the FBI with their investigation." She explained.

"You make a request. Formal paperwork. Then we can help." He said apologetically but firmly.

"Yes; we can do that." She nodded. Had she expected that he would agree to rifle through old receipts for her? She also realized that the request would probably need to be made directly to the phone company and the credit card processing agency. She would need the FBI agent for that. She hoped he would make it a priority.

***

Steve had breakfast at Two Heart's Coffee and walked back to the office. Having stayed longer than usual, he read snippets of the New York Times and the local paper, both of which circulated the coffee shop. The Charleston Post and Courier had announced that Roman Ferrari had been found. His kidnappers had abandoned him in a dumpster in a light industrial park. No ransom note was ever provided and Ferrari had no idea why he had been taken in the first place. Another odd piece of evidence, suggesting some strange screw-up or change of plans. Steve remembered again what the CEO of CTG had said—that Ferrari was supposed to have been kidnapped by environmentalists. What the hell did that mean? Was the Ferrari kidnapping supposed to have been some PR strategy to gain favor for offshore drilling?

Steve wished he was in New Jersey again so that he could retrieve Kenny's laptop and search his emails for any mention of Roman Ferrari, offshore drilling, and Surfers of the Sea. But what would that do? Kenny had been at arm's length from CTG as their outside counsel. If CTG had planned anything nefarious, they probably wouldn't cc Kenny on their email conversations about it; or would they?

But Kenny must have known something. His untimely heart attack seemed like an incredible coincidence. Maybe Rick—their IT guy—could give Steve access to Kenny's computer remotely. Rick had been out sick most of the week—probably had something to do with the coffee shortage. Steve's request would have to wait until Monday, when hopefully Rick would be back. For the time being, Steve would have to satisfy himself mining the law firm's internal server for relevant information. He sat down at his desk and then started looking for memos written by Kenny or any of the young associates at the law firm that might reference Roman Ferrari or Surfers of the Sea. He found nothing, but had an idea.

He had access to the CTG corporate documents obtained for purposes of the litigation he was handling for them. They were barely sorted and represented a massive data sweep from CTG's corporate files based on information requests made by opposing counsel. It would be a long shot that he might find something relevant within them, but why not give them a once look-over? This was an indirect way to access thousands of CTG documents, including emails and internal communications. Many of them would not even be relevant to the litigation. But they may contain something relevant to him now.

He started searching for Surfers of the Sea and ran into a few emails referencing blog articles opposing offshore drilling. It took him another fifteen minutes to figure out that SOS was an acronym for the organization. Searching for SOS, he found two emails. One referenced the offshore drilling campaign in the Atlantic and a related email expressed—in what was barely a single sentence—a need to "discredit" the organization.

Steve had been a litigation attorney for a long time. He knew that such e-mail snippets, which seemed to represent innocent streams of consciousness by corporate employees, could be much more than that. They could be doorways to evidence of corporate ef-ups.

Steve searched for any mentions of Roman Ferrari. Nothing. He speculated it could take him hours to find anything more and maybe there was nothing more to be found. Nevertheless, Steve rolled the email around in his mind. "Need to discredit SOS." How would the kidnapping of a tennis star be used to possibly discredit Surfers of the Sea? And what went wrong? The media had tied the kidnapping to the coffee shortage. Maybe it was supposed to be tied to the Oil Free Oceans campaign, somehow?

And what had Kenny known about it? Not only did he want Kenny's laptop, he decided, but also his phone. It was possible the law firm had paid for the phone and had access to Kenny's messages. Steve recalled implicating text messages he had seen in litigation over the years. He was trying to imagine the sort of text message that could have stressed Kenny out sufficiently to give him a heart attack. Or get him killed.

Chapter 12: Wait, Wait....

Alexis dragged herself down the stairs and into the kitchen. Another day, and she had that Yankee attorney to contend with. She found him rude and abrasive. And she never knew when he was going to barge into her office wanting something. She wasn't used to working on weekends, but he had demanded some "urgent research," which he called her about on Friday afternoon, right before she left for the day. Now it was Sunday and she would have to go into the office to get it done. She opened the fridge and stared inside. Nothing appealed to her, so she closed it again. She then turned on the radio.

Announcer: "For two weeks the country has faced a shortage of coffee. And this week's 'wait, wait, don't tell me' is about the crazy things people have been doing to cope.

Tina is our contestant today—she joins us from Tallahassee Florida. Tina are you ready to play?"

Tina: "Yes I am."

Announcer: "Okay Tina. Here are three news stories and you will need to fill in the detail. You'll need to get two out of three to win. Number One: Programmers at a San Francisco, California software firm went on strike, claiming what?"

Tina: "Uh...their job is too boring to do without coffee?"

Announcer: "That's right! The workers have unionized and demanded that their employer provide each employee with a minimum of one cup of coffee per day from supplies available at the Seattle branch of the same company. The San Francisco-based employees want equal coffee for equal work. Number Two: Italian tennis legend Roman Ferrari announced at a press conference this week that what?"

Tina: "Hmmm....he can't do Wimbledon this year because he's going through coffee withdrawal?"

Announcer. "That's a good one Tina but it's not correct. Roman Ferrari actually announced that his tennis performance has improved since he started drinking the new Luca coffee substitute, which is sold exclusively to owners of Luca's high end espresso machines. Ferrari has been the brand ambassador to

Luca since 2011. Ferrari claims he has had more mental focus and physical energy since he began drinking this proprietary herbal espresso substitute, developed by Stella Coffee in Portland, Oregon. Okay—you ready for number three, Tina?

Tina: "Ready as I'll ever be."

Announcer: "Number three. The Georgia State Legislature has done what as a result of the coffee shortage?"

Tina: "Gone on furlough?"

Announcer: "Yes! The official Georgia State Clerk reported that too many legislative members and their staff have fallen asleep during committee meetings and have called in sick due to headaches and other symptoms of coffee withdrawal. The legislature is on furlough until further notice. Congratulations Tina! You got two out of three!.... Have you been affected by the coffee crisis?"

Tina: "I'm hanging in there but there's a number of people at my office who have been out ill recently or needing extra time to do their work—bad headaches, and that sort of thing."

Announcer: "Where do you work?"

Tina: "I work for a medical device company. We make prosthetics — artificial knee caps are one of our hottest items."

Announcer: "Artificial knee caps? Those are a hot item?"

Tina: "Ugh, yeah—they're in high demand with the aging population of baby boomers. We've seen a steady uptake in artificial knee cap orders in the last ten years."

Announcer: "And how do you order one of those? I mean could I just call your company headquarters and order an artificial knee cap, or do I have to go through a middle man?"

Tina: "Ugh, no...we supply to hospitals and surgical centers. I am pretty sure you need a medical license to order a knee cap."

Announcer: "Well, I guess I would prefer that you and your colleagues take all the time you need making those knee caps. If you need special access to coffee like those software developers in San Francisco, I think you should have it."

Tina: "Thanks, that's very kind of you. We do a lot of quality control on those knee caps."

Alexis turned off the radio and looked blankly around her. She too, was longing for a cup of coffee. It was part of her weekend routine to brew a fresh pot of French roast and read the paper this time of day. Absent-mindedly she filled the kettle of water and turned it on. She opened and closed her coffee cupboard on autopilot, and began rifling through a drawer of ancient tea bags.

'Maybe we should get that herbal espresso blend from Luca for the office,' she thought to herself and made a mental note to talk to the office manager on Monday.

***

Steve stood in the break room, looking for coffee.

"Good morning, Steve! How are you?" Asked the receptionist, in her eternal state of optimism.

"Fine, Carol, how are you?" Asked Steve, determined to stay on Carol's good side, despite his irritation with her relentless good mood.

"Wonderful, Steve. Just wonderful!" Chimed Carol.

"Where's the coffee?" He asked.

"You may have noticed there's a coffee shortage, and the firm is fresh out." Responded Carol. "But we've just put an order for an herbal espresso blend. Roman Ferrari is a big fan of it and he claims it's improved his tennis game."

Steve stood motionless with mug in hand and stared at Carol. Things couldn't be getting worse, he thought.

He returned to his office, wondering how he was going to stay awake during the ocean planning meetings. He would have to parse through what would no doubt be boring dribbles of discussion for nuggets of potentially useful information relevant to CTG's oil and gas interests. He cringed thinking about the coffee withdrawal symptoms he'd heard about on the news. Headaches, muscle pains, lack of motivation, brain fog. He knew that if anyone at the office had any coffee stashed away, they wouldn't share it with him. He was an outsider—a Yankee. He'd have to find his own supply.

Steve grabbed his suitcase and a map of Charleston and headed toward the front door. "Hi Carol," he called to the firm's receptionist, "I'm going out to do some sightseeing!"

"Oh, how lovely, Steve! I'm glad you're going to get out a bit!" Carol beamed at him.

***

Troy Simmons was walking home from work and thinking about the sorry state of his career. After working as a full time IT specialist for a regional bank for six years, he was let go and rehired as a contractor with zero benefits and reduced hours. The whole thing stunk, and he did not know what to do about it.

He walked dejectedly kicking stones along the sidewalk. He imagined they were soccer balls he was dribbling down the field. It was a Friday afternoon and he was thankful for soccer practice early that evening. He needed an outlet for his energies — his head was getting full with self-pity.

He suddenly became aware that a vehicle had been slowly driving behind him. He could feel a sense of alarm mixed with curiosity rising in his abdomen.

Troy turned around slowly. A very large red sedan — what appeared to be a rental car — was indeed following him. There was only one occupant. A guy with greying hair in Friday casuals sat behind the wheel. He pulled up to Troy and rolled down the window.

Troy stopped and waited for the driver. The guy was probably lost. "Hey, do you know where I might be able to buy some coffee?" The driver leaned out the window.

"Coffee?" Troy asked blankly. "You're looking for a coffee shop?"

"No, no," responded the driver impatiently, squinting his eyes half shut. "They're all out of coffee in this town—you know, the shortage?"

"Oh...right. I don't drink coffee, so it's not fresh on my mind."
Troy replied.

The guy in the car looked at him impatiently. "Look, I'm trying
to get my hands on some coffee. Do you know if anyone around
here is dealing in coffee?" He gestured his head toward the street
outside the car.

Troy processed what the guy just said to him. "Around here?
Dealing in coffee?" He asked incredulously. He swung his torso
around and started to walk away.

Steve followed him slowly in the car. "Wait, wait! It's nothing
like that. I'm from out of town.... I just need to find someone
who is selling coffee in this town. It's a high priority for me!"

Troy almost laughed. His meditation teacher would tell him his
agitation stemmed from his employment issues. "Look, I don't
know of anyone who is selling coffee around here or anywhere. I
don't even know why people drink that stuff. It's dehydrating."
He turned and started walking away again.

The car continued to follow at a slow pace. "Hey, I'm sorry," leaned out the driver. "I didn't mean to offend you, and since you're obviously not a coffee drinker, you wouldn't understand. I'm desperate, okay?"

Troy snorted. He turned toward the driver. "So you're out looking for a dealer to feed your coffee addiction? If you run into a drug dealer, you'll probably get ripped off if you're lucky, and get yourself killed if you're not so lucky. Look at yourself! You're going to put your life in danger for a latte? How can you stoop so low?"

"It's not like I'm asking for crack cocaine, okay? I'm a highly functioning individual and I'd like to remain that way. Let me give you my card, and if you hear of anything, I'd appreciate it if you'd pass it on to the right people." The guy pulled a card from the side console and handed it to Troy.

Troy took the card mechanically. "Steve Ledermeyer, Partner. Bailey Carter LLC" Troy read out loud. "You're a lawyer?"

"Yep—although I prefer "attorney." Responded Steve. "And my
work is very intense, you know. I need the coffee for stamina.
Can you help me out?"

"Why don't you just get yourself some ginseng? That's what the
Chinese do—they drink ginseng tea for stamina. North
Carolina's full of ginseng crop—most of it goes to export to
China, though, so we don't hear much about it." Responded
Troy.

"Does it really work?" Asked Steve with interest.

"The Chinese think so. They pay a lot of money for that stuff.
An old friend of mine runs a ginseng farm a few hours north of
here and he swears by it. It's an ancient Chinese remedy.
They've got their own ginseng variety in China, but the
American variety is supposed to be much more powerful."

Steve liked what he was hearing. "I'm willing to give it a try. Can
you get me some ginseng from your friend?"

"Me?" Asked Troy. "Why me? You can just get on the Internet
and order it yourself."

"Well, maybe" responded Steve, waving his hand like he was swatting away a bee. But I won't know what to do with it. I will give you five hundred dollars for a month's supply if you can arrange to have your friend get it to me in some form I can drink without gagging."

Troy wasn't sure how much a month's supply of ginseng would cost but five hundred dollars sounded like a neat sum for selling a bag of herbs to a lawyer. "I'll look into it and give you a call." He responded.

Steve's face lit up. "Great! Just call the cell phone on the card. Er what was your name?"

"Simmons. Troy Simmons. Nice to meet you." Troy gave him his own business card.

"Nice to meet you, Troy. I'm Steve, but you already know that from my card. I'm glad I ran into you. Please call me as soon as possible!"

Chapter 13: Assignments from Above

Jessica Paulson sat in her cubicle on the third floor of a nondescript office building in Charleston. She had been assigned to the regional ocean planning process on behalf of the Port Authority. It would have been a welcome project if it weren't for the fact that Jessica was already overworked. On top of it all, she was in constant battle with Charleston public schools, who wanted her ten year old daughter in a special ed school because she was "hyperactive" and "didn't pay attention to her teacher." The school had issued an ultimatum: either the parents would put Sophie on pharmaceuticals, or she'd be kicked out of the public school system.

Jessica had taken a number of afternoons off recently to talk to the principal, Sophie's teacher, the school psychiatrist, Sophie's primary care physician, and a host of other people who were starting to blur in Jessica's mind. To make up for these afternoons, Jessica was working late hours from home. Then she was up again by 6 am to start work and get Sophie ready for school.

Her husband was away on a string of business trips recently, and was only able to help out here and there. He also had a way of getting very upset about the situation with Sophie—he didn't want his daughter on drugs and was indignant that the school suggested sending her to special ed. This just fueled Jessica into a flurry of activity, scheduling meetings on Sophie's behalf without much apparent effect. She needed more time, she thought, to figure out the situation.

Jessica focused her attention on her work. She was to review her discussion notes in preparation for a presentation at the regional ocean planning process. The words blurred as her eyes teared with exhaustion. The cup of tea she had just finished did little for her concentration. If anything, it made her feel warm and sleepy. It was difficult for Jessica to go without coffee. Maybe she was the one who needed drugs, not Sophie, she thought.

Her phone rang. "This is Jessica," she answered, suppressing a yawn.

"Hi Jessica, It's Doug." Her department director. "How are you?"

"Fine, Doug, how are you?" She replied on auto-pilot.

"Oh, doing pretty well under the circumstances." He said. It had become the standard response since the coffee shortage.

Jessica mustered a weak smile, realizing it would have zero effect over the phone. "I'm just sitting down to look at that regional ocean planning project." She offered.

"Oh good, that's what I was calling about," chimed in her supervisor. "We had a meeting with some of the folks working on the federal level on this, and they wanted to make sure we included in the draft ocean plan an action item about allocating shipping terminal space for oil and natural gas."

Jessica typed in a bullet point with "shipping terminal—oil and natural gas" into her discussion notes. She highlighted it in yellow. "Okay...I've made myself a note to do that."

"Great! Mary's just walking into my office so I've got to let you go..."

"No problem." Replied Jessica. She hung up the phone.

'Oil and gas,' she thought rather blankly, trying to wrap her head around what this project was about.

***

John Warren burst into Jamie's work space at the Pee Dee Research Center. "I have some good news for you, Jamie."

John's face bore a look of deep confidence and satisfaction that Jamie had not seen in some years. "Yeah? What's the news?" Jamie asked with genuine curiosity.

"We've been selected by the International Coffee Organization to research solutions for the coffee mold disaster. I knew you were already working with coffee mold for tobacco, so I wrote up a proposal to them, and they granted the lab 10 million dollars for the next five years to get on this and work on long-term inoculation strategies." John's words rolled off his tongue.

Jamie stared at him in disbelief. "Ten million dollars over the next five years? That's amazing!"

"Yes; and they expect you to lead the project. I'm close to retirement age and ready for the changing of the guard. You're a bright fellow, Jamie, and this is right up your alley. Coffee mold will be your legacy. Mine was tobacco, but coffee is going to be yours. I'm too old to lead a new project. I'll be around to help you for a while, but this is going to be your show from now on, Jamie." He put his hand on Jamie's shoulder like a father would.

"I don't know what to say, sir." Jamie felt rising excitement in his chest. "I'm honored. And a bit dazed. This is huge!"

"It is big news. There are few substances in the world more important than coffee, son. And you'll do right by this, I know." John assured Jamie.

***

That Sunday afternoon Jamie went to his parents' house for dinner. It was his dad's birthday, and the family had gathered from around the state for the event. Chris was there, too, which was important for Jamie. Chris still hadn't paid Jamie back for that boating incident and Jamie was looking for an opportunity to talk to his cousin.

"So how is your work going at the lab?" Asked Jamie's mom.

"Oh, great!" Jamie lit up. "It's actually taken up some major momentum in just the last couple of days. We got a grant from the coffee industry. They are intrigued by our research and want us to apply what we are doing to help them find an antidote to the coffee mold. They are giving us 10 million dollars over the next five years to find a solution to the problem. Not only that, but I'm to lead this project. John Warren is planning to retire and hand over the lab to me." Jamie was beaming with excitement.

Chris' face lit up. "Well, well, Jamie! Look at how successful you are." He crossed his arms and leaned back in satisfaction.

"Wow, that's wonderful, Jamie!" Exclaimed his aunt. She was never super impressed with Jamie's work on tobacco, but the coffee situation was a high priority in her book. "I can't believe I am sitting next to the man who might save America by getting our coffee back! So how long do you think it will take? I hope not the full five years…." She leaned in seriously.

"Well, I don't know." Responded Jamie.

"Does this mean you will get to travel to South America?" Asked Jamie's youngest cousin.

"Maybe..." Jamie hadn't thought about it.

***

Jamie waited until after dessert to approach Chris. They were standing outside in the back yard. "So, Chris. It's been a while. Whatever happened to that money I loaned you?"

Chris scratched his head. "What money?" He stared blankly.

Jamie grimaced with a pained look on his face. "You know, the $300? The boating incident? Didn't you get my voice messages about that?"

"What boat? Oh the booooat..." Chris gained a look of recognition. "Well, I was thinking we could just call it good."

"Call it good?" Asked Jamie incredulously. "Why the hell would I want to call it good? I haven't heard from you for weeks!"

Chris snagged a long blade of dried grass and started to chew on it carefully. "Your recent success at the lab? I guess I had something to do with it."

Jamie's eyes squinted and he screened his forehead with his hand to get a better look at Chris in the blaze of the western sun. "Wha....Did you join the University's Research Department Steering Committee when I wasn't looking?" He asked rather sarcastically.

"Very funny, bud." Chewed Chris. "No. But isn't it such a coincidence that your research is exactly what's going to solve the coffee mold problem?"

"Sorry? I don't get you." Jamie squinted again.

"The coffee mold? That I planted at the Savage Beach Resort?" Chris was back to his favorite topic.

Jamie felt himself turning purple. He could tell he would lose it if the conversation continued; he retreated back into the house and slammed the door behind him.

Chapter 14: Darkness and Light

Marie woke up on Thursday morning from a terrible dream. She dreamt there were offshore drilling rigs appearing in the waters across the globe. There were thousands of them drilling and chocking out life. Her dream was so scary to her that it completely overwhelmed her. She saw a future of pain and death where before she saw a planet of oceans teeming with life. She was sweating heavily.

This was not the first time Marie had experienced such overwhelming dread. Indeed, in the past year she had several dreams where she had woken up in the middle of the night terrified about the destruction of planet earth. Such experiences usually caused her to have an existential crisis for hours. Marie's mind now went over her calendar for the day. One video call in the afternoon and a phone call that morning. Luckily, she didn't need to leave the house. This meant that she could crawl back into bed and recover any time she needed to. That was her only plan, as a cup of coffee was not available to wash her feelings of despair away.

The last time Marie felt this type of dread she was still in Oregon. She was staying with a retired activist on the coast, whom she had told about her nightmares. "You could be right, Marie, that terrible things could come to pass. But remember that the left hand of darkness is light. A famous Oregon author once said that." Marie pondered that advice: remember that the left hand of darkness is light. Did that mean that darkness can only exist if there is light? That light is the left and generally weaker hand? What if darkness is left-handed? That light and darkness are both present in order to accomplish some things? And is darkness also the left hand of light?

It was 6:30 am by the time Marie shook off these thoughts and got out of bed. It was still dark outside but the sun was already coming up. She stood in the house watching the sunrise emerge from the darkness through the window, comforted by the silence.

The following morning, Marie drove over to the Savage Beach Resort to meet Roman and the FBI. She arrived early and filled Roman in on her progress thus far. Roman's wife, Gabriella, was also there.

The FBI agent arrived a few minutes behind schedule. If he was annoyed or surprised by Marie's presence, he did not show it. Sean was his name. He went through the same line of questioning that Marie had taken. Marie listened patiently, keeping an ear open for any new information or recollections from the victim.

At some point, Sean turned to Marie. "If I recall correctly, you submitted information about two young guys who were involved in tainting the coffee supply at this resort immediately before Roman went missing."

"Yes; that's correct." Marie was glad the right people were talking to each other.

"We've been following them but haven't tracked anything suspicious tied to Roman's kidnapping—at least not yet." Volunteered Sean.

"Did you have a chance to look into the cousin at Demson University—Jamie, I believe was his name?" Asked Marie.

"No, not yet; but he's on our list." Replied Sean. He then turned to Roman. "Your unfortunate experience seems related to the coffee shortage. What's the name of the company that sponsors you again?"

"You mean Luca? They make specialty espresso machines." Responded Roman.

"Yes. Is there any chance that they are involved in this somehow?" Asked the agent.

"Are you asking whether they kidnapped me?" Roman was offended by the suggestion.

"Yes." The agent responded, even-keeled.

"No; I don't think so." Roman settled down again. He sat and thought further. "Maybe there's something related to the high profile nature of my involvement in the coffee industry. Someone may have picked up on that and made me a target. I do a lot of commercials for Luca, and I travel internationally as their brand ambassador."

The agent rubbed his forehead. He was probably calculating whether this case would stay in his jurisdiction if the kidnappers were internationals.

"Sean," volunteered Marie. "I ran into another potential lead earlier this week. As luck would have it, I found a Thai restaurant within a couple of miles of a Dunkin' Donuts that did a large take-out for a big guy on each of the days that Roman was missing."

"Okay; that sounds worth looking into." Sean sounded encouraged.

"Should we stay here in town for some time?" Roman asked Sean before he left. "We were hoping to fly home to Italy this week."

"I think you should do whatever you need to do," replied Sean. "Just keep me posted."

After Sean left, Gabriella said she wanted a word with Marie. Roman excused himself for a while. "Marie, I know everyone is thinking this kidnapping has something to do with the coffee supply. But what if it's tied to your offshore drilling campaign?"

"What makes you think that?" Asked Marie, feeling startled by the suggestion.

"The morning before Roman was kidnapped, I had a dream that he'd been taken and tied to an oil rig. It scared me, the images were so vivid and powerful. Later that day Roman was kidnapped right as he was leaving from your event."

***

Marie walked down the beach near the resort after her meeting with Roman, Gabriella, and the FBI agent. She was trying to make sense of what Gabriella had suggested to her. There was no ransom note for Roman. And none of the kidnappers had spoken to him about their motives. Did this have anything to do with the coffee shortage or offshore drilling, or both?

The circumstances around the kidnapping felt so strange—as if it the whole thing was a mistake. Or maybe just a measure to contain Roman temporarily for some reason. What would

Roman have done the following days if no one had kidnapped him? It was a question that neither she nor the FBI agent had asked.

She returned to the resort lobby with the intention of finding Roman again. As she walked in, a headline in the local newspaper caught her eye. "Demson University Awarded Funds to Solve Coffee Mold Problem." She grabbed the paper and read the article. It was about the Pee Dee Research Center and Jamie's lab. And it had a picture of John Warren, the current lab director.

Marie dialed Roman's room. "It's Marie. Are you still around?"

"Yes; where are you?"

"In the lobby."

"I'll be right down."

He appeared just a minute later wearing his tennis clothes.

"Are you in a hurry?" She asked.

"I've got a few minutes." He replied.

"Do you by any chance recognize this guy?" She showed him the newspaper picture of John Warren.

Roman took the newspaper and looked at the picture for a while, his teeth pressing against his lips. "Yes," he said finally. "I saw him recently in Columbia at a coffee plantation."

"What was he doing there?" Marie asked.

"I don't know. I talked to him a little. He told me he was visiting from Charleston and I told him I had just been in Charleston and was going to be back here again."

"You were here in Charleston before, then flew to Columbia, and then flew back to Charleston?" She was trying to wrap her head around what he had just said.

"Yes." Roman confirmed. "I came for my tennis tournament and Gabriella taught a tennis workshop. Then Gabriella and I flew to Columbia. And then we returned here for the Surfers of the Sea event."

"Why did you fly to Columbia?" Marie asked, blinking.

"Luca sent me there. They wanted some video footage of me enjoying coffee out of their espresso maker at the plantations. Their advertising team also wanted to show off the sustainably harvested coffee they support, the fair working conditions, and fair trade practices. I spoke to some of the farm workers on camera — that sort of thing." He replied.

"So you saw John Warren there? While you were visiting the plantations?" Marie sought confirmation.

"Yes. He was there." Roman affirmed.

"Is there anything you learned about him?" Marie then asked.

"Not that I can remember." Roman swallowed, feeling suddenly vulnerable.

"What were you planning to do the days after the SOS event, had you not been kidnapped?"

"Phf"….Roman blew air through his lips. "Do some touring around Charleston, play some tennis. Nothing out of the ordinary."

"Nothing related to coffee?"

"Not besides drinking it, no."

Marie called Sean, the FBI agent, about these revelations. She could tell he was driving when she called. Possibly going back to the FBI regional home office, which was a couple of hours from Charleston. She relayed what she had just learned from Roman.

"Roman Ferrari sees John Warren in Columbia at a coffee plantation. Soon after Ferrari gets kidnapped here in Charleston. The coffee supply crashes from an aggressive coffee mold. Warren is using coffee mold in his tobacco research. Then he gets awarded a lucrative contract to solve the coffee mold problem." Sean summed up the story. "Maybe Ferrari saw something or knows something that is incriminating to Warren?"

"Maybe, but why kidnap Roman and let him go a few days later? What good would that do?"

"Maybe to shake him up a bit. Maybe Ferrari knows something he's not telling us or doesn't want to remember? Or maybe Ferrari doesn't know anything, and Warren just thought he did."

"What about the snippets that Roman overheard from his kidnappers? It sounds like they dumped him because whoever was holding the purse strings got cold feet. Cold feet about what? That does not fit in with the John Warren story very well." Mused Marie.

"That's what he told you, at least. Maybe this is some stunt organized by that espresso maker to get publicity and make an extra few millions? Maybe Warren and Ferrari are both in on it?"

"Why hire me, then? I could get in his way if I got to the bottom of things."

"For credibility, possibly. " He then shifted gears. "You've spent more time with him. Does he seem really shaken up to you, or do you think he could be feigning it?"

"He seems pretty legit to me. Oh, and his wife thinks this might not be related to coffee but rather the SOS offshore drilling campaign."

"What makes her think that?" He asked, now honking his horn. "Geezus…these people need to watch where they're going."

"Premonition." Marie decided not to go into the details of what Gabriella had said.

"I guess anything's possible. Is there any reason why he would be a target in particular?" Sean asked.

"He's a celebrity, standing up against offshore drilling. Maybe someone's trying to discourage him." Marie threw out the idea.

"Have they?" Sean asked.

"I don't know yet." She answered.

"You know, your agency is probably going to get assigned to work on coffee soon. That's the rumor out on the street." Sean changed the subject.

"ATF? You think they'll get assigned to coffee?" Marie sounded surprised.

"Yeah—there's been a number of shady deals around what's left of the existing coffee supply in the States, leading to some gang-related activities." Sean explained.

"Wow; how sad that gangs are getting into coffee—but not surprising, actually." Commented Marie.

"Yep. It's like any other mind-altering substance. Alcohol, tobacco…they're all the same. Drive people to some aberrant behaviors. Not as bad as cocaine and the heavy stuff mind you, but enough to keep you busy." Sean sounded tired all of a sudden.

 "Is the coffee shortage driving you to aberrant behavior as well?" Marie probed him.

"Sort of. I've been waking up the last couple of weeks with severely sore muscles. It takes me hours just to get going. My feet feel like someone's taken a baseball bat to them. And then there's the headaches; they're horrible. That's why I couldn't

visit with Roman any earlier. I could barely move." His voice
was deflated.

"Sorry to hear that. At least you don't look as rickety as you
might feel." Marie tried to console him.

"Thanks." He tried to be cheerful again. "You know, they'll have
to rename your old agency to CAFE. Coffee, alcohol, firearms,
explosives."

"What about tobacco then? You're missing the T." She said,
playing along.

"They're not getting a lot of tobacco related crimes these days,
so they decided to leave the T off." He clarified.

"Oh, brother." Marie groaned. "That actually does sound
better than ATF."

"It's the end of an era. Anyway, I think the Ferrari case will
ultimately be reassigned to CAFE. But for now, let's look into the
Thai restaurant. I'll make a request for the records. Warren's
not going anywhere given his lucrative research contract. We

can keep him on a loose leash for a while." Sean sounded definitive.

"That's fine with me." Said Marie. Then she added, " I should be getting back to my day job, anyway."

"How are you managing to find time for this and your Surfers of the Sea work?"

"A lot of my SOS work runs into evenings and the weekends. And most of the socializing I do is networking. I barely know anyone in town; I just moved here. So I mostly just work in my free time." She admitted.

"I already know most of that, actually. We checked you out quite early on. Just to make sure you weren't involved in the Roman Ferrari kidnapping." He commented.

"I see." Marie replied.

Chapter 15: Alexis Finds Herself

It was Saturday, 10:30 am and Alexis had just arrived at the beach. She wore her favorite lulu lemon tank top — the pattern was something between psychedelic and business casual. She was also wearing cropped yoga pants and her dark blue hoodie half zipped. She took a final look in the mirror in her car. Rummaging through a bag in the passenger seat, she dug out a round compact and swirled some powder across her face. Perfect.

Her motives were more than murky. Alexis had gone on a bad date the night before, leaving her feeling horrible. What made it even more difficult for Alexis was that she seemed to attract boring guys, while what she really wanted was excitement and adventure. A wind of self-pity blew over her, but gradually subsided.

What initially caught her eye when she ran into her date's profile on Match.com was that he surfed. At least he had started to surf. He had recently quit his job in reinsurance for the purpose of finding himself. But it sounded like he was in a panic about his decision and wanted to go back to reinsurance immediately. The industry was all he could talk about during the date.

Alexis had listened politely and was relieved to excuse herself before dessert, pleading that she had to pop into work early the next morning. She then went straight home and locked herself in her apartment. Instead of grabbing a tub of ice cream and turning on Netflix, Alexis was determined to get back on that horse and ride. A burst of energy sent her determined to Folly Beach the following morning. If she wanted to meet a surfer, she would just have to hang out where the surfers were.

She stepped out of the car and walked to the beach purposefully. Her eyes scanned the horizon for surfer types. Alexis saw some guys in the distance out in the water, and a couple of women in wetsuits carrying their boards across the beach. She decided to start jogging. A light breeze blew across her face. It was surprisingly warm, and it felt so good. A thought suddenly startled her out of her bliss. The powder she had just put on her face was surely blowing right off. And she could feel her hair starting to dance in the breeze, despite the effort she had put in to securing it in a cute ponytail. Nevertheless, she jogged on.

She stopped at a particularly scenic stretch of beach. The sun was shining warmly on her ankles and chest. A blond guy was sitting on the beach, leaning against his surfboard. He had pulled his wet suit off to his waist and was basking in the sun. She realized she hadn't planned for what she might say in this moment. Buying time, she started to stretch her legs. "Oh, I'm sorry, I must be blocking your view." She jumped to the side and smiled apologetically at the guy on the beach.

No response.

Alexis raised her voice. "I'm sorry, I must have been blocking your view!"

"Wha?? Ahhh…no problem." He murmured, barely stirring.

"Are you from around here?" She asked, approaching him.

There was silence. Uncounted seconds passed. "I live here. Yeah. Do you need directions?" He responded.

"Me? No. I'm from here too. I was just curious how many people surfing out here are tourists and how many are locals." She responded.

Another long pause. "I don't know. You could take a survey." The guy blinked slowly, like a reptile warming in the sun.

Alexis would have thought he was being rude, save for his sleepy, far off demeanor. She felt beyond awkward and every word was now being dragged out of her.

"Well, enjoy yourself," she flashed him a smile that looked more like a frown and started jogging again in the direction of her car. She was relieved to be away from the situation.

Upon reaching her starting place, Alexis pulled her beach bag from her trunk and returned to plop down in the sand. A woman with a surfboard came out of the water near her.

"Is it cold out there?" Asked Alexis, nodding toward the water.

"Cold? No. It's quite nice," responded the woman. "Pretty toasty in this wet suit. Especially on a day like this."

"Is it hard to stand up?" Asked Alexis.

"Not really. It just takes some balance. Easier if you've done some yoga or ballet." The woman responded and then proceeded to carry her board toward the parking lot.

Alexis put her head down on her beach blanket and mulled that over. I do yoga, she thought. Maybe I would be good at surfing. With that, she promptly fell asleep.

.

When Alexis awoke, the sun was already high in the sky. She got up, grabbed her stuff and walked toward the pier. She spotted a small fortune-telling machine parked outside one of the beach kitsch stores. Alexis produced four quarters from her wallet and shoved them into the machine. A puppet of a wizard became animated inside the glass frame, and the entire contraption started to project the sounds of laughter. A white card spit out of the machine into a small slot — the kind you might find at a subway ticket dispenser. Then the wizard turned himself off, and the accompanying sound effects ended abruptly.

Alexis reached down and picked up the card. "Look inside you for what you seek" was printed on it.

She reread the text, trying to make sense of it. She then walked over and sat down on a nearby bench, suddenly feeling a strong craving for coffee. Unfortunately there was none to be had. Anywhere. It was then that she started to cry. Or rather, weep. Tears poured down her cheeks. She found some tissue in her bag to wipe off the mascara. People passed by, pretending not to notice. She didn't care. Nothing was wrong and yet everything was wrong. Her questionable offshore oil drilling assignment. Steve, the Yankee lawyer. Her non-existent love life. The lack of coffee.

After a good ten minutes of open weeping she put on her sunglasses, crossed the street, and ordered a burrito. She chewed it in silence, feeling her raw emotions soothed with every bite.

"Look inside you for what you seek," she reread the fortune card. "Well," Alexis thought, "if you can't date them, join them." She walked into a surf shop with the intention of renting a wetsuit and board. An hour later, she was in the water.

The following Monday morning, Alexis still had a radiant glow from being out in the sun. For the first time, she did not put any foundation on her face before going to work. She hoped people at the office would comment on her tan so that she could proudly announce that she had been surfing. She skipped the brow pencil as well—somehow it didn't look right without the powder. She walked into the offices of Whyte, Farm & Bellingham feeling refreshed and confident.

"May I help you?" Came the receptionist's voice.

"I'm fine. Thanks, Carol." Alexis responded and kept walking toward the main corridor.

The receptionist stood up. "Are you here to see someone?"

Alexis stopped and turned around. "It's me, Carol; it's Alexis."

"Alexis!" The receptionist came closer, looking at Alexis' face. "Lord, child! I did not recognize you! What a lovely face you've got under there without that make-up! And you've got some color. Good for you!"

"I went surfing," Alexis said weakly, dismayed by the situation.

"It suits you well, Alexis!" the receptionist backed off.

"Thanks," said Alexis and headed for the bathroom.

Looking in the mirror, she wondered, "Do I really look that different?" She studied her face for several moments. Alexis decided she liked her new look, as well as the persona that came with it. She's a woman without time for cosmetics. She's heading to the ocean. She made a mental note to buy a higher SPF sunscreen.

Chapter 16: Ginseng Tea

Troy was sitting at work when his cell phone rang. It was Steve Ledermeyer, the attorney he had met last week cruising his neighborhood.

"Troy! Have you got that ginseng for me? I'm getting pretty desperate over here!" A voice boomed on the other line.

"Why? What's going on?" Troy asked, trying to keep his voice down so as not to disturb the rest of the office.

"What do you mean, what's going on? We're out of coffee and I'm not productive. I'm barely motivated to work. This is a disaster!" Steve elaborated dramatically.

Not being a coffee drinker, Troy rolled his eyes. "Would you be motivated to run out of your office building if there was a fire?"

There was a long pause at the other end. Troy almost thought he'd lost the connection. Finally, Steve's voice came through the line. "Of course I'd be motivated to leave the building. But what's your point?"

"Well, motivation comes naturally when we need it and when it's time. I think you've been regularly using coffee to simulate the body chemistry of someone facing an emergency. You're just going to have to learn to be okay with slowing down and following your natural body rhythms." Troy explained.

It was Steve's turn to roll his eyes. "Okay; I'll try. But when are you going to get me my ginseng?"

"Soon; just give me a chance to do so. I'll get back to you." Troy replied. "In the mean time, you have to figure out how to make it work. Go jogging or something; that should give you more energy."

***

A few days later, Troy gave Steve a call back.

"Steve Ledermeyer." A brusque voice answered.

"Hi Steve. It's Troy. I have a nice ginseng tea ready for you."

"Oh, great! Troy, good to hear from you. When can you bring it by? How about tomorrow morning at 9:00 am?" Steve's voice had softened considerably.

"Ah, yeah, I probably could do that. Where will you be?" Troy responded, smoothing out the paper corners on the bag of ginseng tea he prepared for Steve.

"I'm at Whyte, Farm & Bellingham on Meeting Street near Broad. Fifth floor. Come on down." Steve exaggerated the last sentence like a game show host.

"Let me make sure I got that," Troy was saying, rustling around for a pen. "Okay, this is a law firm on Meeting Street. Whyte, Farm & Bellingham, you said?"

"Yes, that's it. Just take the elevator and come up to the reception. Fifth floor. Ask for me and they should put you through."

***

Promptly at 9:00 am the next morning, Troy approached the receptionist at Whyte, Farm & Bellingham and introduced himself.

"Yes, Steve's been expecting you," She said. Then, turning to someone walking behind him, "Dana, would you mind taking this gentleman over to Steve Ledermeyer's office?"

Dana was a tall Asian woman with a dragon tattoo on her forearm. "Sure," she said, "nice to meet you…."

"Troy — nice to meet you, Dana." They shook hands. Then Dana began walking away, motioning him to follow.

They took a wood staircase that spiraled to the floor below. Most of the lawyer's offices lined the exterior of the building, offering views of the City of Charleston and the Harbor. The interior spaces were reserved for secretaries and other support staff.

"Steve is at the end of the hall in the corner office. If you need help getting out of here, just dial zero from any phone and ask for Dana Wang."

"Thank you, Dana Wang." Troy gave her a slight bow and she couldn't help but smile. He then walked to Steve's office.

Steve was sitting at his computer but saw Troy right away. "I'm so glad you are here!" He got up and greeted Troy with a gasp of relief.

Troy looked around the office, with its spectacular view. "Nice place you have here—you said you were visiting?" Asked Troy.

"Yes, I'm here for a special project. Might be around for a few months. Please, have a seat." They both sat down. "It's a little complicated, so I decided to camp out here with the locals." Steve looked around the room for effect. "I'm from New Jersey."

"I noticed the accent," responded Troy.

Steve was ready for the ginseng. "What do you have for me?" He looked like a little kid at Christmas.

Troy opened a messenger bag and pulled out what looked like a one-pound bag of coffee and set it on the desk. "I worked on this with my friend, Randy—the one who grows the ginseng? We decided that it would be best to blend it with rooibos tea so that it would go well with cream and sugar."

Steve was nodding. "Yes, I'm a cream and sugar guy."

"Oh, and we picked non-stimulating herbs to mix this with because ginseng is powerful stuff—so you don't want to have it with black tea or any other stimulants." Added Troy.

"Okay — I can stick to that." Responded Steve.

"So I wrote down the preparation instructions on the bag. Randy wanted me to let you know that the ginseng is sustainably harvested and the company does not use any pesticides on the foliage, root, or seed." Troy handed him a pamphlet.

"Great; thanks," responded Steve, taking it in.

"There's another thing." Troy added, looking a little sheepish. "You should know this stuff increases male libido."

Steve looked at Troy skeptically. "Does it?"

"Yeah," said Troy, now oddly feeling like the drug dealer he chastised Steve about when they first met. "But this isn't Viagra or anything, so don't expect that. This stuff just raises your energy level overall."

"Okay, fine. I'll keep that in mind." Steve half-heartedly tried to keep a straight face, which made Troy shift in his seat a bit.

"Oh, the check!" Steve exclaimed. "Make it out to?" Steve rummaged through a briefcase and pulled out his check book.

"Troy Simmons. S-I-M-M-O-N-S." Troy watched Steve spell out his name and write $500 in the box. When Steve was done, he added: "Would you mind calling me and letting me know what you think of this stuff? Randy and I are thinking about marketing it more broadly."

"Sure thing—I'll check in with you." Responded Steve, folded his arms, and looked at Troy. "So what's your story?"

"My Story? What do you mean?" Asked Troy, feeling suddenly out of place in the room.

"Well, you delivered this ginseng yourself and now you're telling me you want to make a business out of it. So what's your story?"

"I don't know what my story is yet. I'm an underpaid IT professional at a dead-end job and I just got my hours cut. I feel a lot of resentment about it." He fished around for something more interesting to say about himself. "I enjoy playing soccer in my spare time. I've been taking Zen Buddhism and meditation classes from a Chinese monk for a few years. As a result of my diminishing work hours, I'm now thinking of teaching a class on mindfulness. I'm not really sure about getting into the ginseng tea business. But I like helping my friend Randy—he's the one who owns the ginseng farm."

"Mindfulness class? What do you mean by that?" Asked Steve.

"You know, self-awareness. Being mindful of our internal thoughts and emotions before we react. As well as being mindful of our surroundings and context. And how that all relates to our actions and behavior." Troy suddenly thought about Steve's carefree ability to part with money. "Maybe you would enjoy taking my class." He suggested.

"I'm probably not in touch with my emotions. Or aware of my surroundings, for that matter." Responded Steve. "Except when I'm irritated; then everything bothers me."

"Well, let's say you're irritated. And you want some relief in the situation. Mindfulness will help you figure out the underlying reason why you are irritated so that you can…."

"Usually I'm irritated because someone is acting like an idiot. I just do what I need to get them in line or out of my way." Steve interrupted, dusting his laptop keys with his finger.

Troy looked at Steve skeptically. "Steve, how happy are you with your relationships? With your co-workers, your friends, your romantic partner?"

Steve leaned on his chin and seemed to deflate a little. His thoughts shifted to his divorce. "So what you are saying is that my relationship issues are my own fault?"

"No, I'm just saying that mindfulness can help you really see the situation much more clearly and boost your ability to troubleshoot without having to either get people in line or get them out of the way. Give me an example of something or somebody that is really frustrating you." Troy leaned back in his chair.

"Okay." Steve crossed his arms and frowned in thought. "I've got this PR lady joining me on the case here soon—upon the client's request. I know her from the past and I resent her. She's slippery. She is a human facade and she'll never tell you what she thinks. It bothers me."

"She's probably just looking out for her best interest, like you. She wants people to get in line or get out of the way. Maybe the facade and her evasiveness is her way of accomplishing that. Has that ever occurred to you?" Troy made his case.

Steve chewed his lip. "Can you say more?"

"Sounds like she's got a winning strategy over you." Troy mused. "She knows you can win an argument, but you can't win if she won't provide you with any information. That way she doesn't have to argue with you. In her eyes, that probably puts her in control."

Steve furrowed his brow. "How do you engage with someone who doesn't want to engage with you? I mean, I'll have to be around this woman for weeks or maybe even months. It's got to be bearable and I have to figure out how to be around her."

"You have to make her feel at ease. So she's not pulling away all the time. Just bit by bit, you've got to show her that you're giving space to her and her ways. And you have to become mindful of your attempts to control her—to debate and convince her of anything. You don't want to be doing that, or she'll man up her defenses."

Steve looked at Troy skeptically. "You really think she'll warm up if I make her feel comfortable? How do you know she won't just stay the same?"

"She might, to some extent. But people respond to their environments, Steve. Do you act exactly the same no matter how people treat you? And no matter what is happening around you?"

Steve sat there staring at Troy for a while. "I'll give it a try." He finally said.

***

The next morning Steve woke up earlier than usual. He decided to go for a run along Charleston Harbor, taking Troy's advice to stay active. The sun was already out and sent the promise of a warm day. Steve could not remember the last time he ran outside. He was accustomed to working out at a gym, and usually went at the end of the day, at odd hours such as 10 or 11 at night. It felt exhilarating to be outside and to smell the ocean breeze. Thoughts of his divorce crept into his mind, but he quickly shoved them aside. This was going to be a nice start to his new life.

He returned to his hotel room in a good mood. He was entirely calm and no longer bothered by the fact that today he was to receive Chandra West for a briefing session about the ocean planning process. He showered, got dressed, ate some eggs from room service, and walked over to the office around 9.

It was time for his next cup of ginseng tea. Steve liked the taste of the beverage Troy brought him. At some point the previous afternoon he had a bout of paranoia, wondering whether the tea really contained ginseng and not some random weed or drug.

He pulled out the pamphlet Troy had given him and felt better upon reading it. Ginseng Gardens, LLC appeared to be a family-owned business that had been around for nearly a decade. He carried his tea back to his desk.

Two hours later, Chandra West arrived at the office. ”Good morning, Steve. Good to see you." She shook his hand.

"Good to see you, too." Responded Steve. To his surprise, he was genuinely happy to see her. Chandra's familiar face was respite from the foreign hotel room and borrowed office space that would be his life for the foreseeable future. "Would you like anything to drink?" He asked. “They don't have coffee here anymore, but the firm's got some herbal espresso coming out of their espresso machine."

"No thanks." Responded Chandra, brushing aside his offer. “I've already had my green tea latte. Thankfully I gave up coffee years ago.” She smiled a cool smile.

Steve's eyes glazed over at the mention of green tea. “Okay. Let's dive right in, then." He said.

Chandra took out some papers and began explaining what she needed him to do during the ocean planning process. "You're not going to remember everything," she said after a couple of hours, "so I've created these cheat sheets you can reference later. The key for you, Steve, will be to introduce yourself briefly and express that your reason for being there is to listen. You don't want to get involved with the side conversations and you don't want to become the go-to-guy on corporate plans for offshore drilling. Does that make sense?" Asked Chandra.

"Yes, sure, it makes sense. Hi, my name is Steve and I'm here to learn," Steve said parroting after Chandra. He felt like it was the dumbest thing he could say to introduce himself, but decided it would be best to let Chandra come up with whatever she wanted him to say. And he obviously already knew he was not to run his mouth about CTG—they were his client, after all, and whatever they told him was in confidence.

"That's perfect! Just don't forget to mention that you represent CTG." Exclaimed Chandra. "You just come back to that if you ever feel things are getting out of control."

Out of control? Steve wondered what the heck Chandra was talking about. He considered asking her about the Roman Ferrari kidnapping, but then thought better of it. He straightened in his seat, opting for brooding in silence. Then, feeling the urge to get out of the meeting, Steve leapt out of his chair, exclaiming, "Hi I'm Steve and I'm here to learn. And I'm hungry, will you join me for lunch, Chandra?"

Chapter 17: Ocean Planning

Steve got up for the morning break at his first ocean planning meeting. He thought about how good he had been feeling recently. Was it the ginseng? Was it because he started jogging along the harbor each morning? Or that he traded the hotel in for a short-term apartment rental? He even got into the habit of stopping at a local coffee shop for breakfast. Two Heart's Coffee. It was a quaint place with images of the ocean, and much nicer than his tiny kitchen.

He was now weaving through the crowd of attendees out of the main conference room into a long hallway that had been outfitted with snacks and beverages. He went to the refreshments table and started loading fruit onto his plate.

"Thank god they've brought us some food," came a voice to his right. He turned to see an elderly woman with long, grey hair reaching for the pineapple chunks. "Excuse my manners. I'm Starlight."

"Starlight?" Asked Steve, wondering whether he had heard correctly.

"Yep, that's the name my daddy gave me. Pleased to meet you."
She extended her plate-free hand to Steve.

"I'm Steve. I represent CTG and I'm here to learn." Steve
shook Starlight's hand.

"Aren't we all," commented Starlight knowingly. "Look at this,
for example." She started rifling through an oversized purse, and
pulled out a photo that she pushed into Steve's hand. "Do you
know what that is?"

Steve scrutinized the photo. "It looks like a plant floating on a
piece of plastic." He responded.

"It's a coconut palm GROWING on a piece of plastic. It was
found floating in the sea. You see these coconuts float around in
the ocean and sprout when they hit land. This one sprouted on a
piece of plastic trash."

"Is that possible?" Steve asked with genuine disbelief.

"Not only possible, it is also common. This piece of trash is part
of that great plastic gyre." Commented Starlight.

"The what?" Asked Steve, his facial expression shifting into bewilderment.

"The great plastic gyre. That island of plastic trash, many miles long, swirling in the ocean currents of the Atlantic. It's been there since the 1970's, at least, growing bigger all the time. Disposable plastic bags, plastic bottles, styrofoam, diapers. All these petroleum derived plastic items that don't break down in nature." Responded Starlight.

Steve stared at her in silence, trying to process the information. In the mean time, Starlight fished out another picture from her purse. "You see this?" She handed the second picture to Steve, retrieving the first from his hand. "This is my brother Don wearing his prosthetic leg. He lost his real leg in a tractor accident."

Steve gazed at the picture of an old skinny man wearing a Marlins baseball cap. He was wearing shorts and grinning at the camera.

"That prosthetic leg is made of plastic, too. It's going to last Don a lifetime. And when he passes, it'll probably be recycled into something else—maybe another medical device," explained Starlight. "Unlike those plastic bags floating in the ocean. They just end up in the trash as soon as they're used. Did you know Americans go through twelve thousand plastic bags a second?"

"Twelve thousand bags a second." Steve repeated, feeling slightly green around the gills.

"Yep, hundreds of millions of people getting groceries and buying toothpaste. You do the math." Responded Starlight.

"And you say that this stuff is floating in the ocean?" Asked Steve.

"It certainly is. When I lived on the coast in Northern California, we used to get garbage all the way from Japan. From the tsunamis."

"I don't believe it…." Muttered Steve in a resentful voice.

"You believe it because it's true. Go to NOAA's website (that's the National Oceanic and Atmospheric Administration). They have a whole section dedicated to garbage collected along the coast." Responded Starlight.

Steve handed the picture of Don back to her. "I'll have to do that." He said.

"It was nice to meet you—Phil was it?"

"Steve."

"Oh, that's right—my apologies. My memory is not so good any more." Said Starlight. "You coming to these meetings in the future?"

"I think so," He responded.

"Well, I'll see you around, then." Said Starlight and excused herself.

***

Chandra came out of the ladies room at the Ocean Planning Meeting when her phone rang. She fished it out of her purse and brought it to her ear. "Chandra! What's going on down there?"

It was Carl, the CEO of CTG. "We're just on break, Carl. We spent the first session going through introductions and each participant talked about their stakes in the South Atlantic." As she talked, Chandra spotted Steve off in the distance, who was looking at photographs with an elderly woman.

"I don't give a fuck about the introductions, Chandra! I need you to get in there and situate CTG in the Port Authority's land use plans." Carl yelled into the phone, startling Chandra.

She took her eyes off of Steve and retreated away from the main hall where people were milling near the refreshments. "Carl, I've never heard you so upset." She tried to appease him. "The most important thing here is that we stay calm…"

"Don't fucking tell me how I should feel, Chandra. I'm paying you tons of money to get things done, not to treat me like your my kindergarten school teacher. Get your fucking ass over to the Port Authority rep and do something!" Carl's tone escalated before he abruptly hung up on her.

Chandra was left frowning at her phone, extremely shaken up. She hated when people swore. And she was not used to any of her clients swearing at her. She'd known Carl for several years and he had been nothing but polite to her. But recently, he had shown a very different side of himself. Was it the kidnapping that had put him over the edge? Or was it the coffee withdrawal? Whatever it was, Chandra did not like it. She straightened her suit, put her phone back into her purse, and walked back to the main hall toward Steve.

"Steve, how are you doing?" Chandra sounded more tight-lipped to him than usual. She was wearing a light-colored suit, woven in cream and salmon pink. Her hair was folded and swirled back into something resembling a jelly roll. The skin above her eyelids was powdered white, giving her an innocent and fresh look of a southern belle who had just gotten out of the shower.

"Just fine. How are you, Chandra? Meeting any interesting people?"

"Don't you want to check email to make sure nothing's come through from Alexis or Garett about their meeting this morning?" Chandra ignored his question.

"Oh, right. Steve pulled out his cell phone. "I'll meet you back after the break." He started to walk away from the crowd and parked himself against a wall. He pulled out his phone and checked for messages. Chandra watched until he looked settled. Deciding that he was unlikely to cause any damage while checking email, she went back into the main conference room to chat up the woman from the Port Authority.

Steve was still thinking about the great plastic gyre, feeling a strange heat in his belly. He recognized he had been too busy with his litigation career to ever learn about such a thing, and this threw him off in a strange way. Had she said plastic came from petroleum? He barely had a minute to process all of this before a tall younger woman approached him.

"Hi, you must be Steve Ledermeyer — you represent CTG? I'm Marie Alpern. I'm with Surfers of the Sea." Marie gave Steve an easy smile.

"It is nice to meet you." Steve put the phone in his pocket and regarded the woman in front of him, who looked like she would be most comfortable in a t-shirt and blue jeans. "What brings Surfers of the Sea to the meeting?"

"We're involved in protecting the ocean and the coastline for future generations." She answered in a way that suggested to Steve she had made this statement many times before. She then focused her eyes on his and asked, "How about you?"

"I'm here to listen and learn about the ocean planning process here in the South Atlantic. I represent CTG as an attorney." Steve answered.

"CTG wants access to offshore drilling, is that right?" Responded Marie, holding a benevolent gaze.

"Yes, that is their primary interest." Steve was as level as he could muster. He was not used to talking to anyone beyond judges and other attorneys about his clients.

"Why is CTG interested in this area? I understand there's barely a year's worth of oil and gas in this part of the Atlantic. Seems like very little to make a fuss about, if you ask me. And why the Outer Banks in North Carolina? The entire seashore is a national park. Wouldn't offshore drilling be a bad idea there?" She blinked at Steve curiously.

Steve looked at her with a mixture of caution and disbelief. He had seen some survey maps of oil and gas reserves for the area dating back to the 1970's, but he could not recall the numbers, and even if he did, he would not be able to translate them into supply volumes in his head. "Unfortunately I'm not versed to thinking in those terms. I'm an attorney—I went to law school so that I wouldn't need to do math. Have you asked BOEM about this? They probably can give you the most accurate figures." He was referring to the Bureau of Ocean Energy Management, the federal agency tasked with issuing offshore drilling permits.

"Yes, those figures are from BOEM—we did the calculations, and there's less than a year's supply for the nation out there." Marie replied.

Steve's lips widened into a tight smile. His first instinct was to ask her to check her math. But it was possible she was right. Or there was something she did not know. "I wish I could answer your question for you, but I'm just here to learn. I'm sorry I don't have a clearer answer."

Marie could sense his tension. He seemed genuinely thrown off,
like he really did not know the answer. But he seemed to have an
opinion — one that formed spontaneously while she was talking
to him. Marie thought of the odd look that crossed his face for
just a moment before he swiped it away with his words. She tried
to recreate it in her mind and make it her own so that she could
feel into it.

It was almost as if he were mortified or revolted by what she said.
Marie wondered about this Steve Ledermeyer — he was
confident, as were all attorneys that she had met in similar
contexts. Yet somehow he seemed like a fish out of water.
Maybe this wasn't his regular gig, she thought. She decided to
change the subject.

"Oh, before I forget! We're having a special reception this Friday
for participants of the ocean planning process. She reached into
an envelope under her arm and pulled out a flier, handing it to
Steve. "Sydney Hamilton, the marine photographer will be
there, along with an exhibit of these amazing photos he took last
fall of North Atlantic Right Whales. It starts at 6 pm at Two
Heart's Coffee over in the French Quarter." Marie was not in

the habit of inviting oil and gas attorneys to Surfers of the Sea events, but her gut instinct told her it was the right thing to do.

"I know Two Heart's. I've been having breakfast there regularly." He then paused and skirted around her invitation, "I'm not sure I can make the event, but I'll try."

"There will be wine and appetizers from one of the local restaurants. Charleston style. It should be a lot of fun! I hope you can make it. Feel free to bring a date or come solo." She added, then excused herself.

"Okay; thank you." Steve gave a light laugh at the prospect of bringing anybody to this party. Outside of work, he had not met anyone who lived in this town other than Troy.

***

Chandra received another phone call from Carl just as she was coming back to her hotel room that evening. She heard sniffles on the other end. "Chandra! Honey! I'm so sorry I yelled at you earlier. It's just been this coffee thing. I admit, I'm a total addict, and the withdrawal's been getting to me."

"Okay." Said Chandra. The explanation did not make her feel any better.

"How did things go with the Port Authority rep?" More sniffles from Carl. Had he been crying? No, it didn't sound like it at all. The sniffles got more intense.

"It's going to take a while to establish a relationship, Carl, but I plan on continuing to talk to her regularly. She seemed somewhat distracted but receptive to what I had to say." Chandra focused on giving Carl a report that would calm his nerves.

"Okay; great! Keep going at it, sweetheart! You're my babe over there; don't let me down." She heard a clamor at the other end as Carl struggled to put the phone down on a table. Then the line went blank.

Babe? Sweetheart? Honey? She wondered, and stood there in silence for a good long while, not knowing what to make of yet another strange change in his behavior. Had he been sniffing cocaine? She needed a drink, she decided, and headed back out of her hotel room to explore the streets of Charleston.

Chapter 18: The Right Whales

The next day, Steve was back at the office looking through Kenney's files on offshore drilling. What he was finding troubled him. He learned that CTG had been bought out two years ago by a large chemical manufacturer and that the parent company was pushing for offshore drilling in the Atlantic. He thought about Starlight and the great plastic gyre. What if the purpose of drilling in the Atlantic was not to fuel cars but rather to manufacture plastics?

Steve went back to his CTG litigation repository of documents and searched around for evidence of plans to extract oil for plastics manufacturing. To his surprise, he found chemical industry projections that plastic production would skyrocket in the next decades. The same report stated that the chemical industry was snatching up oil companies across the country. Other reports noted that many of these same companies were building manufacturing infrastructure along US coasts for plastics manufacturing. Offshore drilling would be their main source of supply.

He checked on the offshore drilling reserves data that Marie had asked him about. There were several maps in the database, including a few prepared by the military. Indeed, there was less than a year's worth of oil and gas in the region to supply to the US as fuel. He wondered how much volume that was in terms of plastics. He turned to the one source everyone does when they don't know the answer: the Internet. A few short and agitated clicks later, he concluded that the volume could potentially be huge. He would need to get more information.

He then remembered Marie's question about oil and gas drilling interests in the Outer Banks, North Carolina and looked at the maps again. There were no special reserves demarcated for the Outer Banks. "Hmm…" He sat back in his chair. What special opportunity was there for CTG and possibly other oil and gas companies in North Carolina and the Outer Banks in particular? To the extent these companies had some political connections there, these had obviously not worked out for them. Who would want to drill in a national park, anyway, and why?

Steve stood up and paced around his office. He was unable to obtain Kenney's cell phone data—his IT guy told Steve that Kenny's phone was his own. It was too bad. But a picture was emerging nevertheless. One that he didn't like. The oil and gas reserves in the Atlantic could be more lucrative than he imagined and they were being tapped into for the purpose of making disposable products that would pollute the oceans. He sat back in his chair and took a deep breath.

It occurred to Steve that he needed to call Troy back about the ginseng tea. He found Troy's card and dialed his number.

"Troy? It's Steve, calling you about the ginseng tea."

"Hi Steve! How are you?" Troy answered enthusiastically.

"Fine! Look; I like the tea and I think it's doing a world of good for me. I'd like to know if you can get me more." Steve got to the point.

"What do you think about a monthly subscription?" Troy asked, thinking about how this could be a viable business.

"Okay; great! Let's do that! I'd like to secure my supply for the future, because you never know." Steve responded.

"No problem; we can make you a priority."

"We? Does that mean you're officially getting into the ginseng business?" Steve asked.

"Well, I don't know." Replied Troy. "I'm still hoping to teach people how to live a mindful life."

"Seems like a great time to do that, Troy. I bet there are thousands of people in this town right now having a meltdown because there's no coffee. You could really help them." Steve was encouraging.

"You think so? But I don't even know how they feel. I've never had a coffee addiction—or any other addiction for that matter." Troy commented.

"That's precisely the point. You are a walking miracle to them. You could teach people how to navigate life without coffee." Steve offered.

Troy was silent for a while. "I guess you have a point." He finally concluded.

"Troy, do you have time for lunch this week? How about tomorrow?" Steve sounded insistent.

"Lunch? Why do you want to have lunch?" Troy was wondering where this was going.

"I need to run some thoughts by you. Consider it your first private mindfulness coaching session. It's my treat and I'll pay you for your time. Do you like seafood?"

***

The waiter had just placed a pile of scallops in front of Steve. Troy dug into his plate of lobster. "I'm used to questioning people for work — during depositions and in court, you know?" Steve bit into a scallop and chewed thoughtfully. "But I don't have a good track record of getting info out of people outside of that context. When I ask people why they're acting a certain way, they get offended. When I tell people that they're doing something wrong, it either leads to an argument or their refusal to talk to me." He admitted.

Steve was thinking about his soon-to-be ex-wife. He felt like some sort of accessory to her. The husband who escorted her to parties and fixed the sink; a convenience that helped maintain order in her life. But the passion and intimacy were gone. Not knowing what else to do, Steve accused her of being cold and aloof. When this didn't work, he would point out things that were wrong in the world, hoping to get some emotional reaction from her. The homeless man living near their apartment; didn't she care? She ignored his attempts to get through to her, lips pursing into a tight frown as she disappeared behind her cell phone.

"Telling someone you don't like something is not the same as telling them what you need. They're miles apart." Troy commented. "When you criticize people, they'll often shut down. They feel hurt and they don't know what to do instead."

Steve worked the muscles of his face. "What if you know that they're not interested in your needs and priorities?"

"If you truly know that, then there's nothing to talk about. You won't know, however, unless you ask. At least state what it is that you need from them, rather than criticizing them." Responded Troy.

"What are you supposed to do if they don't want to talk — like that PR woman I told you about?" Asked Steve.

"If you need them to talk to you, then you have to tell them that you need them to talk to you. And always focus on what you need. The topic of what you think they are doing wrong is none of their business." Troy advised him.

Steve sat up, trying to grasp what Troy was saying. "Okay; I think you're telling me that I should focus the conversation on me and what I need, rather than focusing it on them and what they're doing." Is that correct?

"Yes! I think you've got it Steve! You know, I think there's a sensitive guy inside of you that wants to come out. He just hasn't had much time in the sun yet." Troy smiled at Steve encouragingly.

"It's interesting you say that because I don't think I'm a sensitive guy at all, but my wife…er ex-wife…told me on occasion that I'm overly sensitive."

"A lot of men are sensitive by nature — they've just been conditioned to suppress that. It's not considered manly enough. Then they have a hard time in their personal lives because they don't know how to express how they feel."

"What do you mean when you say that they have a hard time expressing how they feel?" Asked Steve, dumbfounded.

"They don't ask for what they need directly because they fear the repercussions of being vulnerable. So they criticize others instead so the focus stays on someone else. They bottle up their emotions and blow up later when that bottle gets too full."

Later, as they were leaving the restaurant, Steve remembered something else he wanted to ask Troy about. "If a person wanted to do something questionable and most people objected to their idea, why would that person keep trying, especially if they had no particular financial benefit from doing it?" Steve asked, thinking about the Outer Banks and offshore drilling.

"Why would they keep pressing on?" Troy considered this. "Maybe because they had a vision and because they told some people they could make it happen. Maybe they'd feel like a fool or a failure if they didn't come through." Troy mused.

Steve listened carefully. "I see."

***

By the time Steve arrived at Two Heart's Coffee Friday evening, the place was full. He located the bar and ordered a glass of wine. No tables were open, so he started to walk through the crowd. He settled on an area from which he knew he would be able to see the speaker.

"I'm doing a presentation for SOS here next week Sunday on hormone disrupting chemicals and how they're affecting crocodile habitat in Florida." He heard a voice nearby.

"What are hormone disrupting chemicals?" Asked another voice.

"They're toxic chemicals used in many consumer products. They disrupt the normal functions of hormones in humans and animals alike. People think of hormones as just sex hormones— but they control everything from fetal development to our energy levels," said the first voice.

"Where do they come from — these chemicals?" The second person asked.

"Many of the toxic chemicals used by industry come from petroleum." The first voice responded. Steve felt a sense of frustration creeping in. What didn't come from petroleum?

They were then called to attention as Marie introduced SOS and Sydney for his presentation. Steve focused his eyes on the shy and well-tanned photographer on stage. He looked like the type of guy Steve might find changing out of a wetsuit in a public parking lot. Steve was surprised to hear that he had been observing Atlantic right whales in a manner that would likely impress any marine biologist. Steve was also surprised to hear about the Atlantic right whales, whose existence had largely escaped him up to just a few days ago. He could feel his throat tightening with emotion as Sydney described their demise.

Sydney also mentioned the plight of dolphins, whose numbers were dwindling as well.

After the main event, Steve stuck around to have tapas and mingle with the crowd. There were a variety of locals from the Charleston area, including environmental activists, real estate agents, and small business owners. Most of them seemed to already know each other, and he felt like the odd man out.

"Hi Steve; glad you could make it!" Marie greeted him warmly as he found himself drifting out of a conversation about oysters.

"Thank you; I'm glad I came." He replied courteously. Then he switched modes. "How is that tennis player doing; the one who was kidnapped? Do you know him from Surfers of the Sea?"

"Oh, he's doing pretty well, I guess. Shaken up, as you can imagine. It's a very unpleasant experience to go through." Marie responded.

"Are there any ideas about what happened?" Steve asked.

"Well, there might be some connection to the coffee mold problem. Although it's possible it had something to do with his connection to our offshore drilling campaign." Marie tried to be as frank as possible.

"Why would someone kidnap him over the offshore drilling campaign?" Steve made an effort to sound neutral.

"I don't know, really. I can only speculate." Marie admitted.

Chapter 19: Chandra's Dilemma

Chandra stood in the ladies room at Whyte, Farm & Bellingham. She was thinking about an argument with her brother just a week prior, when she was visiting him for the long weekend. It was a repeating argument, really, which had gone on for years. Her brother thought that Chandra had sold herself out by working in PR, and that she had turned her back on her working class background.

Chandra accused him of being a hypocrite, since he too had moved away from their home town and had sought to erase all traces of his humble origins with his upscale townhome and expensive car. "At least I know who I am, Chandra, and I take care of my own." He had stared at her. The implication was that Chandra had sold out to corporate interests.

She probably would have brushed this off as she had brushed off similar comments from him over the years. But everything felt different now.

She had gotten used to working for people who kept their emotions under wraps. If they were angry or frustrated, they didn't show it to her. Everyone had been polite and courteous and had complimented her on her work well done. This had all changed since the coffee shortage.

She was now witness to temper tantrums, violent outbursts, and binges of anger from corporate executives and other PR people. She felt shaken up and abused. People would eventually apologize, blaming it on the lack of coffee. The excuses did not make Chandra feel any better, however.

The worst thing about these outbursts is that they made people's motives self-evident to her: they were ruthless in pursuing their own petty interests. They wanted to maintain the appearance of superiority even when they had obviously screwed up, to preserve their investment when stock prices tanked, and to maintain control when things were obviously out of their control.

It now occurred to Chandra that people were ruthless before the coffee shortage; this just wasn't self-evident. And because they were so flattering to her, she had easily convinced herself that they were kind and civil. But really, they were not.

Chandra looked at herself in the mirror. Was she ruthless as well? Instead of seeing herself, she felt like she was staring at the face of someone else; someone she didn't recognize well. As if the eyes and soul she gazed upon didn't match the eyes and soul she expected. The person in the mirror is the one Chandra strived to become. The person viewing the mirror was someone else, someone surprised at the outcome. Her own image frightened her and all she could do was avert her gaze and return to her office.

She was barely out of the ladies room when Steve ran into her with what seemed like excessive cheer. "Chandra; I was just looking for you! I'd love to try dinner at a place by the water that Alexis recommended. Can I invite you? We can discuss the case over some food and fresh air."

Chandra really needed fresh air, and nodded in agreement. "Yes; I'd love to," she confirmed. "Let me just grab my purse."

They walked out together and strolled through downtown. The air was warm and breezy; the sun was low. Most people had left their offices hours ago and were out enjoying the evening. There was a collective air of leisure and festivity from the streets of Charleston.

"So, do you think we have a good chance at this offshore drilling thing?" Steve asked as they crossed a cobblestone street. "It seems like we are in some troubled waters. I'd love to hear your opinion."

Chandra had a lump in her throat from her image in the bathroom mirror. "Honestly I think if people knew my opinion, they wouldn't want anything to do with me." She surprised herself; why had she said that?

If Steve was thrown off by her response, he didn't show it. "How can you live without expressing what you really think?" He said offhandedly, looking around the street for the restaurant.

"I'm not paid to express what I really think. You know that, Steve. I've built my entire career on information management." She retorted drily.

It occurred to Steve that the conversation was way out of character for Chandra. He stopped walking and looked at her. Her eyes seemed to challenge his gaze.

"I think this is the place." He finally said, ushering her toward the restaurant.

They entered and were seated on the outdoor patio. The two of them took their time looking at the menus and getting situated. Steve waited until after they ordered to start a conversation about what was on his mind.

"Okay, let me ask you: what kind of shit fest did I inherit from Kenny by getting involved in this case?" Steve got right to the point.

Chandra stared at him for a while, thinking. "I don't really know the details, Steve. I was just brought in a few weeks ago to steer things in a better direction."

"What did they tell you?" He folded his arms impatiently.

"About as much as you seem to already know." She replied, pursing her lips. "I don't really need to know all their dramas in order to do my job."

"Okay; what happened to Kenny?" He asked her.

"I thought he died of a heart attack." Chandra looked at him somberly.

Steve's confidence in getting any information out of Chandra waned. Nevertheless he pressed on. "I guess the general creepiness of that phone call with Mr. CEO made me wonder how we all got here." He unfolded his arms and leaned in toward her. "The one about the kidnapping." He whispered dramatically.

"I think some people did a foolish thing before we got here, Steve. Now it's our job to get this ship back on course." Chandra smoothed the table cloth with her hands.

Steve took a sip of water, swooshing it around in his mouth. He was realizing that he, Steve Ledermeyer, did not personally like the course he was being asked to steer toward. But he wasn't ready to tell Chandra he didn't believe in offshore drilling.

"Seems like CTG is in a pickle over this Roman Ferrari incident." He stated, unfolding his napkin and arranging it neatly on his lap.

Chandra looked at Steve inquisitively. "What do you know about it?" She finally asked.

"Well, I know they screwed up—a PR disaster you called it. And they're not making any headways with the offshore drilling thing. I'd say the situation is out of their control, don't you think?" He leaned his arms back against his chair.

Chandra sniffed mildly. "I think we're here to work on the offshore drilling matter now." She steered the topic in another direction.

Steve became quite frustrated by her evasive reply. "Oh, sorry—I forgot you're not paid to give your opinion." He had never been good at controlling his irritation. And deep down inside he hoped that his terseness would crumble her facade.

Just then the food arrived. They both stayed silent as the waitress laid out small dishes of meat, rice, and an assortment of vegetables. Steve served Chandra a sampling of everything and then did the same for himself.

"So what happened Chandra? I deserve an explanation, don't you think? I got stuck on this case, and I need to know how deep it is." Steve was getting insistent.

"Okay!" Chandra exclaimed, holding her forehead with the side of her hand like Steve was giving her a headache. She looked around the room and then leaned in toward Steve with a lowered voice. "Someone at the company — I don't know who — decided it would be a good idea to kidnap the tennis player, tie him up to a bridge and wrap him in an anti-offshore drilling poster created by Surfers of the Sea. They wanted to smear the organization to have a better chance at the South Atlantic Ocean Planning process. She leaned back with a deep frown and dabbed her napkin against her lips.

"I knew it!" Steve exclaimed a bit too loudly. Then he lowered his voice and started over. "I knew it! I knew there was something fishy and that it was tied to discrediting that organization." He exclaimed with satisfaction. "So they wanted people to think that Surfers of the Sea kidnapped the tennis player. And make them look bad. But why did CTG pull the plug on the plan? Did Kenny find out? Did it have something to do with the coffee shortage?"

"My understanding is that the kidnapping was reported in the news as being associated with the coffee shortage and it took the wind out of their sails. And CTG's legal department found out about the kidnapping because they accidentally learned of a very large sum of money that was used to pay for the job. Their General Counsel threatened to resign and that put an end to things." She folded her napkin. "I don't know what happened to Kenny or what he knew about all of this; I'm sorry." She added apologetically.

Steve sat there in silence chewing his lip, trying to sort through the story. He imagined that if the General Counsel confided in Kenny, the situation could have stressed him out sufficiently to cause a heart attack. "And you didn't know about this until afterword?" He finally asked, scrutinizing her.

"I did not know." She replied and fell into silence, looking away.

Steve studied Chandra for a while; as if looking for evidence of her honesty. She seemed sincere.

Chandra met his eyes a few minutes later. "I know what you're thinking," she said. "You're thinking all this PR stuff has undermined my better judgment and that I've lost my integrity. Actually, I lost track of the real me before I even got into PR. That's why it was so easy for me to be good at this job." She looked down at her food in disgust with herself, wondering why she was telling this to the man sitting across from her. Because she knew he wouldn't tell anyone else, she concluded.

"I wasn't thinking that." Steve chewed thoughtfully on a piece of steak. A number of thoughts came to his head but most of them were not very flattering. He remembered what Troy told him about not criticizing people and said the only thing he could think of that would not make Chandra feel worse. "I don't know whether it's possible to lose yourself. I mean, there you are, just sitting right there."

She smiled ever so briefly at that. "But the real me feels hidden somewhere. Not really accessible anymore. " She insisted. "Maybe not even to me."

Steve had been observing Chandra as much as possible since she had arrived in Charleston, trying to understand the woman assigned to his project. He liked her better when she was not paying attention to him or anyone else, absorbed in her own private thoughts. Her face would soften—even if she was wasn't smiling.

He wanted her to know this but did not want to tell her he had been staring at her. What would Troy want him to say in this situation? Something assuring, but what would be assuring to Chandra? He didn't know, but decided to say something about what he had seen in her.

"I hate to tell you this Chandra, but the real you is still accessible to me, and everyone else who is not asleep on this planet," responded Steve. "It's most visible when you're not looking." He took the opportunity to stuff some rice into his mouth.

"It's visible when I am not looking?" Repeated Chandra, trying to understand.

Steve chewed for a while, and at the risk of talking with his mouth full, explained, "Yeah. When you finish a sentence or look down at your papers, or look away. There's you all over your face. You just can't hide all of that. You haven't scripted your down time."

Chandra straightened up and rearranged herself. She cleared her throat. "And what do you see?"

"I'll tell you, if you first tell me why you feel the need to walk around like your on camera." Responded Steve.

"Well," replied Chandra with a sigh. "I guess it's worked for me professionally. I change my colors to satisfy my clients."

Steve scrutinized Chandra for a while, working through a broccoli floret. "So being a chameleon has been an advantage to you."

"Yeah." Responded Chandra. She looked around her. "So how about you? You have almost the opposite approach to life. You seem to have no trouble telling people what you think." Chandra blinked at Steve with a benign look.

"That's my job." Responded Steve. "To tell people what I think. As long as I don't think too hard." Steve started rubbing his eyes.

"What do you mean by that?" asked Chandra, surprised by Steve's answer.

"Well," Steve paused, "I'm paid to say what I think, but I have to tow the company line. Companies like CTG pay me to advise them on what they want to hear. You and me aren't all that different in the end, Chandra. We both stick to the script. Your script might sound more smooth than mine, but we both stick to the script." He was surprised at himself for making that comparison.

Chandra was taken aback by his answer. She gazed at Steve in silence, deciding how to respond. "Well, I guess we have something in common." She finally replied.

"I guess we do," he said almost cheerfully.

"So what do you see in me when I'm not looking?" She asked him again, biting her lip.

"It varies." He admitted. "Today I see a frustrated woman who seems unhappy with the current situation." He wondered how he could steer the conversation back to offshore drilling.

"It seems like people have become so uncivil ever since the coffee shortage." She finally lamented. "But maybe they were always uncivil and I just didn't notice."

"Kidnapping a tennis player seems pretty uncivil to me." Steve blurted. "That seemed to have been planned way before the coffee thing." He chomped on a marinated cucumber with what seemed like great pleasure at what he had just said.

"I just don't know what to believe any more." Chandra ignored his comment. She had something to get off her chest. "Up until recently, I thought showing emotional restraint was some sort of virtue. It made you able to communicate effectively and get what you…get what needed to be done." She wanted to say, 'get what you want,' but that didn't sit well with her. "Now the same people who seemed so virtuous to me have turned into yelling tyrants and they blame it on the coffee shortage."

"No one likes to be yelled at, Chandra. But you have to admit, sometimes people have good reason to be mad. And they're just trying to express those reasons—even if they're doing it badly." Steve was thinking about his imminent divorce. A wave of sadness came over him.

"What?" Asked Chandra.

"What do you mean, what?" Steve asked defensively.

"You're obviously sad about something."

He knew he owed her his honesty, given that she had been honest with him. "I just finalized my divorce papers. The conversation made me think of that." He stopped chewing and propped his chin on his fist. Then he decided that keeping his elbow on the table in a southern restaurant was rude, and put his arm away again.

"I'm sorry Steve." Chandra looked at him sympathetically.

"Thank you." He blinked away. "What I was trying to say is that there's some passion behind people's anger. You've got to get to that underlying passion to understand people."

"I know that now—I think." Said Chandra. It was her turn to put her elbow on the table as she propped up her forehead. "But the passion underneath some of the people around me is not a good kind of passion — it's just…ruthless." She again said the word she had been rolling silently around in her mouth for the last hour.

"How ruthless?" Steve asked, thinking of Kenny.

"I don't know. Just ruthless — not in anyone's best interest. Not the companies', not the people's best interest — it's just some ego thing." She drank some water to cool her thoughts.

"Like with CTG, for example?" He prompted her as he would prompt someone at a deposition.

"This goes beyond CTG," she replied. "It's the whole industry."

"You mean the oil and gas people?"

"Yeah, I guess. That's what I've been doing for so long—oil and gas." Her lips sunk into a tiny frown.

"You know they're into chemicals, too?" Steve was thinking out loud.

"What?" She looked like she had just swallowed a frog.

"You don't know that? The industry is consolidating. They're moving away from energy production to plastics. It's looking more lucrative these days." He found it hard to believe that was news to Chandra.

"Ah, yes, I did know that. I just didn't think much about it before." She replied, looking uneasy. "I knew about the plastics thing but I didn't really think about the consolidation with the chemical industry as much." She explained.

"How does thinking about it now change things for you?" He asked, sensing her discomfort.

"Just reminded me of something from my family. I'll tell you some other time." She was playing with her water glass.

Chapter 20: The Warren Inquiry

The FBI's investigation of Chris, Tucker and Jamie had absolved the trio from any connection to the Roman Ferrari kidnapping. This did not surprise Marie, as the three of them didn't seem organized enough to orchestrate something that sophisticated. The kidnappers seemed more like professionals to her; possibly ex-military. Nevertheless, it was possible that John Warren hired these guys to kidnap Roman.

Because Sean, the FBI agent who met with Roman, was in too much physical pain from coffee withdrawal to travel to Demson, Marie agreed to push the Warren investigation forward. She pulled up to the main parking lot at the Pee Dee Research Center and gave John Warren a call.

"John? It's Marie Alpern. We have an appointment?" She spoke into her cell phone.

"I'll be right there." John's voice sounded distracted. A few minutes later, he arrived and offered her a strong handshake.

They walked through a maze of grey corridors to a small laboratory-style office. John invited her to take a seat next to a stack of papers and field equipment. "You said you're investigating the Roman Ferrari kidnapping?" He asked.

"Yes; I wouldn't bother you about it, except that Roman recalls meeting you some weeks prior during a coffee tour in Columbia." Marie said in a friendly manner.

John's eyes had a bit of a deer in the headlights look for a moment, and then he relaxed again. "Oh, yes!" He finally said. "We did meet! I don't think I'd ever met a famous person before —that was a first." He was gushing with excessive enthusiasm.

"What were you doing in Columbia?" Asked Marie.

"I was on vacation. Well, admittedly all of my vacations are a bit work inspired. You see, we've been utilizing research into coffee mold to help understand tobacco mold. So I couldn't help myself but schedule a plantation tour. Talked to the managers about the coffee plants. As I recall, Roman and I sampled some coffee together." He sounded as innocent as could be.

"Seems like it paid off — I hear your research lab just secured a major contract to help solve the coffee mold problem." Marie commented.

"Oh, yes, well…that's for the next generation to deal with. I made my career in tobacco and I'm ready to retire in a couple of months. It will be up to Jamie to tackle the coffee mold challenge. But you're right — we were at the right place and at the right time with our research during these otherwise unfortunate times." He looked like he was done with her. "Is there anything else you wanted to ask me about?"

"Did you get any financing yourself from the contract?" Asked Marie.

He shook his head and pursed his lips. "The contract went entirely to the University and this lab."

Marie was somewhat disappointed by his response. She expected the contract would be a giant windfall for John Warren personally. But it turned out he was exiting the scene. Maybe the Warren-Ferrari connection was a mere coincidence after all.

Nevertheless, she made a mental note to ask the FBI to look into Warren's finances.

"I have to ask you this, if you don't mind: is there any reason at all why you may have wanted to kidnap Roman Ferrari or have him kidnapped?" She stared directly at John, waiting for a response.

"Why on earth would I want to kidnap a tennis player? Just because I saw him on a trip somewhere?" John Warren looked genuinely bewildered at the question.

"Well, he is brand ambassador to Luca espresso machines. And you are working on coffee mold here, and you were in Columbia looking at coffee mold." Marie felt sheepish even as she was saying this. The connection sounded tenuous.

John Warren looked at Marie critically. "So?" He finally asked.

Marie cleared her throat. "What do you plan on doing after retirement, if I may ask?"

"Sitting on a beach in a straw hat with one of those tiki huts nearby — you know, the ones with the grass roof? I always wanted to sit next to one of those, but I've only seen them in photos. Do you have any recommendations on finding a nice blue water beach with one of those huts nearby?" He asked her.

"Not really; sorry I can't make a recommendation." She answered.

"Too bad. Well, if you'll excuse me, I have some things to take care of this afternoon." He politely invited her out of his office.

Marie looked for a reason to stay at the research center longer. "I'd like to talk to Jamie before I leave; could you point me in the right direction?"

John frowned slightly, but didn't argue. "Certainly; let me take you over to his lab." He walked her through a few nondescript hallways and rapped at a door where Jamie was sitting on a stool. John then took his leave and Jamie received Marie in the space that he had inherited as the new lab director.

"Congratulations; I hear you are the top dog of this place now." Marie said warmly, trying to dispel any bad blood that may have arisen between her and him from the Ferrari investigation.

"Thank you; I try not to think about it too much and just focus on the research. Otherwise I'd get too overwhelmed." He couldn't resist a proud smile.

Marie looked around at the petri dishes on the table. "Jamie, did anything strange happen—or did anything go missing from the lab—around the time that John took his extended vacation some months ago?"

Jamie frowned. "Not that I know of. Everything seemed pretty normal to me."

Marie couldn't believe she drove all the way out here for this. 'I guess I did my due diligence,' she thought; nevertheless, she was disappointed that there were no leads. She made small talk with Jamie for a while and then excused herself. She decided to at least stop for a hike in one of the state parks before heading back to Charleston.

She phoned Sean at the FBI on her way back. "I'm pretty sure that guy had absolutely nothing to do with the Roman Ferrari kidnapping." She reported. "But you might want to look into his finances and see whether he's benefitting from the coffee mold problem. He claims he's not benefitting from the industry contract, but you never know."

"I won't be able to do that, Marie. I just got news that the FBI doesn't want to pursue this matter and that this case is being transferred to CAFE. They are taking over anything related to coffee. And I've been taken off the case" Answered Sean.

"And what are the chances that CAFE is going to take action on it?" Asked Marie, a bad feeling coming over her.

"Honestly, very low. They're too busy dealing with street gangs selling caffeine poppers laced with cocaine. Apparently it's their new business model. Attract customers with caffeine and get them hooked on cocaine." He remarked.

"What about the Thai restaurant? And Roman's kidnappers?" Did you learn anything from the phone records and credit card inquiry?" Marie wanted to know, ignoring this piece of street news.

"I was able to trace the phone records back to a military contractor who left the country last week. He's been stationed on a work assignment in the Middle East. I've documented it all in my file." He answered apologetically.

"So this case is being transferred to another agency because it's coffee-related and the prime suspect left the country. It sounds to me like this investigation is quickly falling to the bottom of the priority list," Marie thought out loud, biting her lip.

"Sorry I couldn't help you more, Marie." Sean offered. "It's out of my hands now."

"What about John Warren? Maybe someone could check into his bank accounts? What if he had something to do with the coffee mold?" Marie insisted.

"We discussed that at an informal briefing yesterday. CAFE's totally overworked and not interested. If the press got wind that John Warren was a suspect in the coffee mold crisis, they would possibly take down the lab. And then we'd be left with no coffee and no coffee mold research. It's just too messy politically, Marie."

"I see." She said.

***

Marie met with Roman a few days later to explain the situation.

"I'm sorry Roman, but it's going to be hard to follow up on this guy. He's somewhere in the Middle East for a legitimate employment and we don't even know whether he was involved. Although my gut instinct tells me he was."

"I see." Roman nodded with a degree of resignation. He put his hands in his pockets. "Gabriella and I are flying back to Italy at the end of the week. I can imagine we will be out of sight and out of mind."

"You're probably right, unfortunately. There are going to be jurisdiction issues since you're a foreign citizen and this guy left the country. You might need to speak to someone in the Italian government to get help." Marie looked at him sympathetically.

"I'm just going to have to help myself in the end." Roman drew out a deep breath. "I might not be able to find these guys, but I can prevent this from happening to me again." He said resolutely.

"What do you plan on doing?" Marie asked.

"I have a friend who has wanted me to join his martial arts studio for a while. I guess this is the time to do so. I need to learn to defend myself going forward."

***

The next day Jamie was in the break room with Kevin Barrett, one of the graduate researchers in his lab. "Kevin, I noticed you checked out one of the portable cooling units a couple months back. Was that for the greenhouse studies?"

Kevin reached for the refrigerator and pulled out a bottle of kombucha from the collection stockpiled on the bottom shelf. "I didn't check out any cooling units — we haven't been doing anything new in the greenhouse for some time—just cultivating the same strains." He took a swig and looked at the bottle with genuine appreciation.

"Well, you are listed as checking out one of the cooling units in the log book—about the time John Warren was on vacation." Jamie insisted.

"No — couldn't have been me. Must be someone else." Kevin shrugged. "Why; does it matter?"

An uncomfortable feeling filled the pit of Jamie's stomach. After Marie had left yesterday, he had remembered to look at the laboratory log book. Someone had written in that Kevin had checked out a portable freezer for several weeks during John Warren's vacation. The notations in the log book didn't particularly look like Kevin's handwriting. But it didn't look like John Warren's either.

Jamie had then looked at the inventory of petri dishes in the central lab refrigerator. One petri dish of the most virulent strain of the coffee mold was unaccounted for. Jamie counted and recounted them. He checked whether it was mistakenly sorted into another bin; it was not. This, and the checked out cooler had troubled him. He had waited for an opportunity to talk to Kevin.

Now he felt Kevin was waiting for a response from him. "No, I guess not; don't worry about it, Kevin. You didn't take out one of the petri dishes with the most virulent strain of the coffee mold by any chance, did you?"

"No. I've only been working with the tobacco hybrids. Why, did something go missing?"

"I'm not sure yet; just trying to account for everything. Make sure we're sticking to good lab practices with the transition." Jamie tried to brush it off.

Kevin emptied his kombucha bottle and threw it in the recycling bin. "Okay; I've got to get back to the greenhouse. See you later."

Jamie went back to his office and sat down. A host of disaster scenarios began to fill his mind. He visualized John Warren, portable cooling unit in hand, traveling to South America and other places to spread coffee mold around the plantations. Why would he do that? For the $10 million contract? What did he have to gain if he was about to retire? He searched in his mind and remembered John grumbling about the University's bad investments and the state of his retirement fund. He mentioned he didn't think he could afford to enjoy his retirement as a result of the mismanagement. All of that had changed—somehow.

Could John have contaminated the coffee supply? No; it was just a natural disaster. But how could it have come on so quickly and consistently around the globe? Jamie felt bewildered and tired.

Should he call Marie and tell her about his suspicions? What would that mean for his coffee mold contract? The future of his lab would be ruined. Or would it? It was not his fault if his predecessor caused the problem. But nevertheless, he would have to take the blame. And then there would be no money, no coffee research, nothing.

"I shouldn't jump to conclusions," Jamie thought. It would be disloyal to report his supervisor for potentially checking out a cooler, especially when he didn't even have evidence that his supervisor was the one who logged out the cooler in the first place. Sure, a petri dish went missing. But it could have been any of the other lab staff. And maybe they were just experimenting with something for their research. He was probably making mountains out of mo-hills.

Chapter 21: Ice Cream Floats

Brigg and Marie sat down at the cafe to take a break from their preparations. All morning they had been running around, getting Two Heart's Coffee ready for the Ocean Planning Ice Cream Social. Brigg had been concerned that the Nescafe he would be serving with ice cream and porter beer would attract unwanted and uninvited guests. As a result, he and Marie had spent the morning putting up curtains on each of the windows, and two sets in front of the entryway to obscure what was going on inside.

They were aware of the high level of personal desperation many people had reached around the coffee shortage, and felt a lot of anxiety about it. Just a few days ago a group of people had broken into the Folgers industrial roasting facility and stolen the remainder of their supply of freeze dried coffee. This piece of news shook up both Brigg and Marie, and they wondered whether they were getting themselves in way over their heads.

Marie had already issued the invitations for the event, however, and they knew there was no going back now. At the last South Atlantic Ocean Planning Meeting, she handed out fliers one by one to everyone in attendance, asking them to keep the event on the down low. She also instructed everyone — both in person and in the flier — to mention to others that this was an event for participants of the ocean planning process only.

"I think it would be good if we announce early on that this is the last of the coffee you have." Marie said, thinking ahead.

"Good idea. I also suggest we repeat that fact on a regular basis as we are serving people so that they will remember." Added Brigg.

Marie nodded, then asked, "Did you put the sandwich board sign out?"

"The one about this being a private event? Yes; I have two of them and put them both out. One next to the front door and one next to the street corner." Brigg assured her.

Marie started biting her lip. "God, I hope nothing goes wrong." Apprehension clouded her face. "I'm so sorry I got you into this, Brigg!"

"It was my idea, remember?" Brigg laughed at her nervously. "You can't pin this one on yourself."

"I know. But I also know you are doing this because you like me." Marie gave him a guilty smile.

"Oh, you noticed?" Brigg feigned surprise and put his arms around Marie.

She held him closely, telling herself everything would be okay.

***

Jessica convinced her husband and daughter to go to the ice cream social with the promise of sugar and coffee. They arrived early; nevertheless they stood in line outside of the coffee shop for nearly an hour to get their treats. Everyone there was on their best behavior, as if any rudeness would destroy their chance at getting access to sugar and caffeine. Her husband ordered a shot of Nescafe over a scoop of vanilla ice cream; her daughter a chocolate ice cream in a waffle cone.

Jessica herself went straight for the full ice cream float: porter beer, vanilla ice cream, Nescafe. It was hot and she felt nervous and hollow. Marie had invited her to the social during the last South Atlantic Ocean Planning meeting, handing her a flier about the speaker on hormone disruptors. Jessica had never heard of hormone disruptors until a week before that.

She had been sitting in an unmotivated heap at the Port Authority's Planning Department, pretending to work on the South Atlantic Ocean Plan. At the time, she considered leaving and driving home but instead started surfing the web, realizing that she would use up half a vacation day if she took off early.

She searched for information about her daughter's ADHD and came across a research paper that linked childhood diseases such as ADHD and autism to hormone disrupting chemicals. Most of the article was a blur of academic jargon peppered with an alphabet soup to describe a handful of chemicals the researchers referred to as hormone disruptors. She skipped to the end where the researchers concluded that these chemicals increased the risk of "neurodevelopmental disorders" in children. Including ADHD.

The article pulled Jessica out of her stupor. With a burst of new energy, she searched for more info. Other research articles came up of a similar nature. And yet she had never heard of hormone disruptors. Not from her pediatrician nor the ADHD parents group she had joined.

Jessica pulled out her cell phone and started messaging parents she knew in the ADHD group in Charleston. "Have you heard of hormone disruptors?" She asked one woman. "No, why?" Came the response. She asked about a dozen other people and no one had heard of them.

Now Jessica found herself vying for a table at Two Hearts Coffee up front near the speakers. The cafe was filling up quickly. Indeed, by the time Sophie finished her ice cream, the room was packed with people standing all the way to the back wall. Jason, her husband—like many other adults in the room—was sitting back with a buzz caused by the long-awaited jolt of caffeine. Jessica took another swig of her beer float and pressed her cheek against the cold glass.

It was obvious to her that half the people in the room were only there for the coffee. She herself would normally never show up at an event like this, and would have politely declined it. She was busy enough with work during the week, and did not want to attend weekend educational events; she had her family to take care of and needed a break from her job. Even if she were to go to something like this, she would never be able to get her husband and daughter to come along, either. She knew many other people felt the same.

But the coffee shortage and speakeasy-style dole-out of Nescafe at this event had created a buzz of excitement usually not to be found around public planning efforts.

The room was full; people were laughing and joking. It felt more like she was attending a music performance at a bar than an afternoon science lecture. The woman at the table next to Jessica was on her second cup of Nescafe. She was talking loudly and excitedly. The man sitting at the table behind her was asking his companion what the presentation was going to be about.

Marie stood up soon after and said a few words about SOS and the Oil Free Oceans Campaign. Then she introduced the main speakers, a former field researcher of Florida crocodiles who owned the coffee shop, and a toxicologist from Demson University.

The field researcher talked about abnormalities in crocodile hatchlings from hormone disruptors that they were exposed to in the womb. The toxicologist talked about the impacts of hormone disrupting chemicals on human health. She did not talk about ADHD or autism. Nevertheless, the idea that her daughter's health could have been compromised while Jessica was still carrying her as a baby nagged at her.

The speakers also mentioned that many hormone disrupting chemicals came from petroleum. This caused Jessica's stomach to turn. The thought of having oil and gas drilling be included in the South Atlantic Ocean Plan suddenly bothered her. She started to feel depressed about her work for the Port Authority, which was keen on permitting oil and gas terminals in the Charleston area.

After the presentation and Q&A, Jessica went up to the toxicologist and waited patiently in line to talk to her. There were two people already there, asking her about plastics and specific chemicals used in their formulation. Jessica felt upset, and could not pay much attention to what they were saying. Most of it was scientific jargon she wasn't familiar with anyway. Jessica waited patiently until the other people departed before introducing herself to Lorie Rubin.

"Hi Lorie, thank you for that presentation. My name's Jessica. I have a personal question for you. My daughter has ADHD and I was wondering whether that could be caused by hormone disrupting chemicals." Her lips were pursed into a thin line.

"It's nice to meet you, Jessica. Yes, there is a link between hormone disruptors in consumer products and the rise of neurodevelopment disorders such as ADHD." Lorie replied. "So it is quite possible."

"I see." Answered Jessica. "Are there any advocacy groups for parents around this issue? Or any non-profits I could tap into to learn more?"

Lorie looked at her sympathetically. "There are some national organizations that are concerned with hormone disruptors in general but I'm not sure whether any of them advocate on behalf of parents of kids with ADHD. I'm sorry I don't know more about that."

"I see. Thank you." Jessica responded blandly.

***

Steve stood in the back of the coffee shop during the presentation. He wondered how many people had turned up just for the coffee; he estimated it was about half the room. He spotted Chandra in the crowd, and she nodded to him briefly, a frown slowly creasing into her lips. He would have to explain himself later, as he hadn't mentioned his plans to attend this event.

After the Q and A, Steve headed over to the ice cream service. He was careful to avoid Chandra as he weaved through the crowd. Marie sprung up on Steve just as he was finishing his vanilla ice cream. "No coffee float for you?" She asked.

"No; if I had some coffee now then I might be pining for caffeine for the next month." He smiled at her with a deep smile that creased his eyes and cheeks. Steve was proud of having shifted to drinking ginseng tea, and decided he had no plans to return to coffee, even after the coffee crisis was over. He felt much calmer and more energized on this herbal alternative.

"About half the people here are saying that; the other half want seconds." She gave a light laugh and then got serious. "Did you have a chance to look at the maps of offshore oil and gas reserves for the Atlantic again? I'm curious if you have any new thoughts on that."

"I haven't seen anything different in those maps than what we discussed last time." He replied slowly, watching her brow furrow into a perplexed crease. "But I have a question for you." He added.

"Yes?" She asked, wondering what he might want to know from her.

"Where did the speakers say plastics come from?" He asked in his most innocuous manner.

Marie thought about this for a moment. "They're produced from the waste products of oil and gas refining."

"Are they?" He asked, sounding intrigued.

"Well, at least that's where conventional plastics come from."
She couched what she had to say.

"Oh, I see. Isn't that interesting." He stood there staring at her
as if she was supposed to comprehend something important from
this.

"You mean, this is about plastics?" She asked, somewhat
surprised. "They want to drill for oil and gas to make plastics?"

 "Well, thank you so much for hosting yet another highly
enjoyable event, Marie!" He ignored her question. With that, he
slipped away and disappeared.

Chapter 22: The Confrontation

The following Thursday evening Chandra confronted Steve for going to the SOS social without her permission. "You didn't tell me you were going to the party." She stated matter-of-factly, leaning on the door frame to his office. She had returned the day before from business meetings in Washington DC.

Steve was packing up for the night. "If I did, you would have told me not to go; but I wanted to." He replied and pretended to look for something buried in his briefcase.

"You mean you would have listened to me?" She asked, sounding surprised.

"I wouldn't have had any choice, would I?" Steve didn't look up.

"There's always a choice." Chandra lowered her arm.

"When did you get philosophical?" He got up from his desk, finally looking at her.

Chandra ignored the question and moved closer to him. "Now that you went anyway, what did you learn?"

"I learned that this is a shit project and it is no wonder that Kenney had a heart attack working on oil and gas permits for CTG." He responded a bit loudly.

Chandra shut the door to Steve's office. "You're going to have to elaborate on that response." She said to him in an even-keeled voice.

"Come on, Chandra. You can see as well as I do. We might as well be advocating for clubbing baby seals. Doesn't it bother you?" He was almost yelling now.

Chandra felt his anger reverberating in her chest. "So you're becoming an environmentalist now?" She sat down across his desk.

Steve followed her cue and sat back down next to his computer. "The only reason I was not an environmentalist before is because I was an ignorant asshole. What's your excuse?" He regretted saying that as soon as it came out of his mouth.

"I think we'd better get out of here before you make a scene."
She lowered her voice and stood back up again.

She led him through the streets of the French Quarter navigating
slowly through narrow alleys and stone sidewalks. "Where are
we going?" He finally asked.

"I need a drink," was all she could say in response. He followed
her obligingly, mesmerized by the boiling cauldron of emotion
under her voice. It was not an emotion he thought he would
ever witness from her.

They may have walked another ten minutes or twenty. He
wasn't sure. He admired her determination and was concerned
for the state of her feet in her high heels. If they bothered her,
she didn't show it, but rather plowed on through the evening
light. She finally stopped at a narrow building sandwiched
between the rest and told him this was the place she intended for
them to go. He followed her in.

It was a cozy place with bright cushions buffering the customers
from the hard wooden benches pressed against the walls. A jazz
band was playing and an imposing woman was singing to the

crowd. A number of couples were dancing on the make-shift dance floor, which partially served as the official way to the bathrooms. Chandra headed to the bar and ordered the only thing on the menu for both of them: a cocktail with fresh-squeezed grapefruit juice and vodka.

They eased onto a bench and set their drinks on the table. He watched the crowd and listened to the band for some time. The whole scene was vibrant and alive. He was stunned by the contrast between the blank wall Chandra usually wore during the day and the environment she had just invited him into. It was as if he had suddenly stepped into her internal world and it was a place he never even knew existed.

He turned his attention back to her face. She had almost completely downed her cocktail by then. "So what are you trying to prove, Steve?" She asked, looking slightly less put together than he remembered.

Between the music, the people, and the decor around him, Steve completely forgot what they had been talking about. "What do you mean?" He suddenly noticed his own drink and gave it a sip, and then another one. It tasted refreshing in a way he did not expect. "This is good! The band is good, too." He added.

Chandra glanced over at the band and back at Steve. "You pretty much told me you're not on board with this project." She slumped against the bench.

"I know this project may be important to you," Steve began, making some effort. "But I'm not tied to these people and certainly not to this environmental permitting stuff. And I think it's a load of crap." He vaguely recognized that — to the extent he had intended to do so — he had largely deviated from making Chandra feel at ease.

"Look, Chandra. I knew nothing about this ocean planning stuff a few months ago. I thought what we were doing was right and we were the smartest people. But it turns out we are just upper class tools for the oil and gas execs and we've all been absorbed in making money at the expense of the entire planet."

Chandra looked away from him and closed her eyes as if she had just witnessed someone jump off a bridge.

"What? What's that look about?" He asked, taking another sip of his drink.

She wouldn't reply. She just sat there, looking somber.

A minute passed and she still didn't say anything. It was as if something had lodged in her throat and she was recovering.

He decided to give her more time. His eyes wandered back to the musicians. He sat there listening to one song, then another, then another. Chandra still hadn't said anything — she just played around with her glass.

Steve couldn't wait any longer and let out what was on his mind: "Look, we're trashing the oceans and we're doing it for the convenience of the oil and gas industry. Dolphins are dying from our pollution, Chandra—these are intelligent, sentient beings. And what do we get for that? Plastic bags blowing around in empty parking lots and other plastic crap that we don't even need."

Chandra looked pained and searched around the room for some condolence. There was none to be had, so she settled on nursing her glass in silence.

"Can I get you another cocktail, Chandra?" He asked, looking at the last inch of her drink still sitting in the glass.

"No; thank you, Steve." She said. She blinked a few times. "Do you think we could taxi back? I think I need to sleep on what you said."

"How about getting some dinner before you head home?" He asked.

"No thank you."

***

They sat in the taxi as it weaved through downtown. Steve was thinking about apologizing to Chandra when she finally spoke. "Do you know what you want to do next?" She looked at him directly now.

"No, not yet," he answered, wondering whether she was arming up some PR campaign in her head that he wanted to steer clear of. "But I'm not in a hurry." He hoped that gave her enough comfort to leave things be.

They pulled up to her rental apartment and he told her he would take care of the cab. She nodded and stepped out. "See you tomorrow."

Chandra walked into her apartment and shut the door. Dolphins are sentient beings. Had he really said that to her? The client was paying for their drinks, their cab ride home, their housing, their flights to Charleston. None of this seemed to particularly phase him. For no apparent reason he had spilled these feelings out to her, even though she was the last person on the planet he should be talking to about the incongruity between his personal values and those of his client.

She was the PR strategist for the oil and gas industry, for God's sake. Her job was to identify dissenting opinions and annihilate them. She could call the company's CEO right now and have Steve pulled off the project. Even make sure that he and his firm never worked for another oil and gas company again. But she knew she couldn't do that.

Steve's mutiny was like a personal slap in the face. It burned with the memory of her father, who had tried to stand up against corporate interests and lost. She had watched him go down in flames and be crushed by the forces he tried to stand up against. She wanted to stop her father's physical and emotional fall but there was nothing she could do. She vowed never to let what happened to him, happen to her.

The only sure way she knew how to do that was to climb the professional ladders presented to her. The more disinterested and independent she could stay of humanity's problems, the safer and more secure she would become. As such, Chandra did not feel anything when she thought of the environment, even though she was very much aware of the environmental destruction caused by her clients. She had distanced herself from the world's problems so that she would not have to be touched by them.

Chandra was in a conundrum. In her efforts to create security for herself, she had worked her way up to become one with the

forces that crushed her father. Her brother was right; she had
sold out. She had never fully faced this reality before. The
current realization about the consequence of her choices
pulsated within her body, causing her to feel hot and nauseous.

Now Steve — a man she had previously considered to be
completely disinterested in the plight of the world — was
wanting to save it. She didn't think it was humanely possible for
such a complete turn-around to take place. And the fact that it
had just occurred in Steve Ledermeyer, corporate attorney,
shocked and stunned her.

She could not fathom what would make him slow down enough
in his daily routine and career ambitions to notice the actual
problems in the world around him. Truth be told, she felt like
she hardly knew Steve before this project, even though she had
participated in meetings with him for years. He had been just
another suit to her, next to the countless of others she had
interacted with in the course of her career.

This project was becoming a turning point in her life, and she
didn't quite know where it would take her. But she knew for the
time being that she could have an influence on the outcome of

the offshore drilling proposal for the Atlantic, and Steve's wake up call was meant to be a wake-up call for her as well.

***

The next morning there was a knock at Steve's office door. It was Chandra. "Have you decided whose side you're on?" She shut the door behind her.

"You're asking whether I've changed my mind from last night? No, I haven't. I've seen what there is to see here, and I'm not going to go along with it." He crossed his arms with determination. "How about you? What side are you on?"

Chandra's face looked slightly pained. "If you hadn't talked to me last night, I wouldn't have taken a side. But now I realize it's impossible not to be on one side or another. I know you're right about the environmental issues. I have known that all along — even before you were aware that there was any problem. But I had no reason to do anything about it. It wouldn't have done me any good."

"What do you mean, you knew?" He asked.

"I mean I knew. I've been there before — on the other side. I grew up in a town that was destroyed by profit-hungry corporations. I've witnessed water pollution, sickened children, and adults dying of cancer. I knew I didn't want it, so I chose to climb my way out of there so that I could be on the other side drinking clean water and breathing fresh air.

Steve stood up and looked out the window, considering this. He wasn't sure what was more tragic; her knowing a victimized world and disassociating from it, or his ignorance of human misery. He cleared a growing lump in his throat. "Where did you grow up?" He asked.

"The Upper Kanahwa Valley in West Virginia." Chandra looked at her hands as she spoke. "It's one of the most heavily polluted parts of the state due to the chemical companies. My mother worked at one of the plants and died of cancer. My father spent the rest of his life organizing the community and fighting for the company to clean up its act. It never did and he died of a heart attack a few years later."

"I'm sorry, Chandra." Steve was suddenly angry with himself. "People like me don't even know that this stuff is happening. I grew up in a leafy suburb outside of Washington DC." He cleared his throat. "Went to a private high school. Drove a Corvette. Worried about becoming captain of the debate club and whether I'd make it in time for soccer practice. I'd never seen anything outside of that, really."

She looked at him with as much of a smile as she could muster and looked away again. "That's how I wanted my life to be."

Steve rubbed his face, giving it a good exfoliating scrub. "I'm sorry we're living like this, Chandra." He finally said, and turned to look at her.

He suddenly felt tired of the facade he was used to wearing every day: the bubble of intellectual stoutness and cynicism he projected around himself, designed to pre-empt the world and anyone in it from fooling or deceiving him. So much of his energy went into preventing others from getting close to any aspect of him that could potentially be naive or disappointed.

A smoky sensation curled around his Adam's apple and began to solidify into an uncomfortable pressure. It occurred to him that he— like Chandra—used a facade to navigate his career. Only his took on a different form from hers.   This realization took the wind out of his legs and he sat back down at his desk.

She looked at him unaware of the universe of consciousness that had just traversed his physiology. She was chewing lightly on her lip. "It's best we let them take themselves out." She finally said.

"What do you mean?" Steve stirred from his thoughts.

"There's sure to be something they've been doing that wouldn't sound very good if it made it to the front page of the paper." She replied.

"You mean, like kidnapping?" He asked.

She batted the idea away as if she were shooing a fly. "No; something much easier to attribute to them. We're looking for classic white-collar crime stuff — like bribery."

Chapter 23: The Whistleblower

Being a PR person sometimes means using subversive ways to gain info. Later that day when Steve went out to get lunch, Chandra went back to her office and hacked into CTG's email system with a 'special service' used by some in her industry. She narrowed down her search to the email accounts for upper management who had emailed anyone in state, regional, or local government in South Carolina related to offshore drilling and the South Atlantic Ocean Plan.

Four hours later, Chandra found an email. It was from Doug Amos at the Port Authority to CTG's Director of Regulatory Affairs, thanking CTG for the ocean-side home they gifted to him in North Carolina and restating his commitment to help CTG secure its interests in the South Atlantic Ocean Plan. The recipient of the email thanked Doug for his continued support and noted that the company was "counting on him." Chandra couldn't believe her luck, as she half-expected to be grasping at straws in her research.

Now there was the matter of how to bring this email exchange to light without involving either her or Steve. She got up from her chair, stretched, and looked out the window. The image of Jessica Paulson came up in her mind. She was the Port Authority staffer assigned to sit in on the South Atlantic Ocean Planning meetings. A few internet searches revealed that Jessica Paulson reported directly to Doug Amos.

Chandra sat back down at her computer and pulled up Jessica's email account at the Port Authority. She scrolled through emails about Jessica's work and private life. There was an email to a friend expressing frustration at the Charleston school system for not accommodating her daughter's ADHD. Jessica wrote that advocating for her daughter felt like a full time job and sometimes she was so drained by it that she felt like quitting her work at the Port Authority.

Chandra searched through all of Jessica's emails that contained the term "ADHD." She found a recent email from Jessica to her husband, attaching a research article that implicated ADHD with hormone disrupting chemicals found in plastics. Jessica's email asserted that plastics were manufactured from petroleum refining. Chandra sat back in her seat and clasped her fingers behind her head. She knew that for all intents and purposes, Jessica Paulson was the perfect choice.

Chandra picked up the phone and dialed Jessica's cell phone number, which she found in one of Jessica's emails. To her surprise, the woman answered her phone.

"Jessica, you don't know me, but I am a good samaritan. I have evidence that your boss has been taking bribes from an oil company to approve their plans for offshore drilling. I have emails going back and forth between them."

There was a pause on the other line. "Is this about the South Atlantic Ocean Plan?" Asked Jessica. Chandra could hear street noises in the background, imagining Jessica was on her way home, maybe picking up her daughter from school.

"Yes it is. It is about the South Atlantic Ocean Plan." Confirmed Chandra. "I will send you the emails shortly to your work account."

"Wait," asked Jessica, sounding disoriented and confused. "But why me? Why send them to me?"

"Who else is there, Jessica?" Chandra said to her. She then hung up the phone.

***

Jessica got home and gave her daughter a glass of juice from the fridge. She was thinking about the phone call she had received earlier, wondering whether the caller had already sent her the emails she had been talking about. Or was the call simply a practical joke? She felt strangely self-conscious standing there in her house, as if she was on stage. Although she made it a point not to fiddle on her cell phone while she was with her daughter, she pulled it out anyway, while the girl sat cross-legged on the floor.

Jessica flipped through her work email, scanning the subject lines. "Our phone call" stuck out and her heart rate seemed to speed up a little. That must be it, she thought. The sender was "Charlie's Angel." Jessica quickly forwarded the email to her personal account and moved the original to her "SAOPP" folder, which was short for South Atlantic Ocean Planning Process.

"Sophie, honey, do you want to watch baby Yoda while mommy does some things on her computer?"

***

She had googled "what happens to you if you become a whistleblower" and the reality didn't look so good. Namely, you lost your job and couldn't get work in your industry again. Jessica thought things over and was ready for that outcome when her husband got home.

"Honey, Sophie's about to get thrown out of public school because of her ADHD and I thought I would stay home for a while with her. It would cost us half my salary to send her to a proper private school and I just cannot swallow that. Plus, I think I am about to get fired." She bit her lip, approaching Jason.

"Fired? Why on earth would you get fired? Is it because you've been taking so much time off for Sophie?" Jason stopped searching the fridge to look at her.

"No it's not that, Jason." It's just….um…look: my boss is taking bribes from an oil and gas company and I'm about to become the whistleblower." She said bravely, and went on to explain the situation in great detail.

"Jessica, honey, you're not going to get fired. You work for a public agency. The worst they can do is transfer you to another department. If you really want to stay home with Sophie, tell them you need paid time off to process all this." Jason downed his glass of juice.

***

Jessica waltzed into the office a half an hour later than usual the next day with a turmeric latte in hand. It didn't taste very good to her, but at least it was something. She felt pissed. The more she thought about her boss, the more pissed she got. Here she was, diligently doing her job for the Port Authority, raising her child, dealing with the school system, and running a household. All she expected in return was that others be reasonable with her. And yet, here was her boss, abusing his Port Authority power to get beach-front property up in North Carolina.

Jessica had fueled her anger way into the morning, when she decided to forward her boss' emails to the Charleston Post and Courier. Now a strange anxiety sat in, as all she could do was wait. Trying to do her job now felt like walking through molasses, but she chose to push through anyway, turmeric latte for company.

She barely got three pages into writing a report about the harbor's cargo ship capacity when her cell phone rang. "Hello, Jessica? This is Joe Fuller. I am an investigative reporter from the Charleston Post and Courier. Is this a good time for you to talk?"

"Yes," Jessica answered into her cell phone trying to sound calm. "Let me just step outside." She grabbed her purse and headed for the door.

The next day it was in the paper:

Port Authority Employee Taking Bribes from Big Oil: Doug Amos in Deep DooDoo

> Emails show that Doug Amos of the Charleston Port Authority has been accepting bribes from major oil company CTG, which has its eyes on the Port of Charleston as a staging area for offshore drilling in the Atlantic. Offshore drilling is off limits in the Atlantic,

but companies like CTG are trying to change all that.
In a move that no-doubt was meant to circumvent a
federal ocean planning process for the South Atlantic,
CTG paid off Amos to help secure its interests. The
department head accepted property in coastal North
Carolina in exchange for a promise to support favorable
terms for CTG in the South Atlantic Ocean Plan. The
emails were revealed by a junior staff member who
works for Amos, and claims to have obtained them from
an anonymous source who calls herself Charlie's Angel.

Jessica put down the paper and called her HR department.
There was no way she was going into work that morning.

***

Jessica and Sophie got home that evening much later than Jason
did. "Where have you two been? Have you seen the
newspaper?" He asked.

"I saw it first thing and called HR. They told me to stay home.
Well, I did and then I got a message from one of the parents in
the Facebook group: Christina. She's been researching the

hormone disruptor thing for some time. Well, anyway, she home schools her son and we went over there." Jessica was nearly breathless as she spoke. "She and I really hit it off and we decided to start a non-profit to help parents like us with ADHD kids."

Chapter 24: Cleaning the Deck

Marie read about the Port Authority scandal online. It came as a daily email newsfeed about all things oil and gas related to the Atlantic Coast. She forwarded the article to the Chair of the Charleston SOS Chapter and SOS Headquarters.

Although she was not doing policy work for SOS, she had seen enough of her colleagues in action to know that this was an opportunity to appeal to the South Carolina legislature and ask them to take a formal stance against offshore drilling.

Several emails and phone calls later, she was drafting a formal appeal letter that SOS employees, volunteers, ocean friendly businesses and partner organizations could send to their state representative and the governor in opposition of offshore drilling. The letter highlighted the underhanded tactics used by the oil and gas industry to set up shop in the state, referencing the CTG scandal.

Within a few days, thousands of people had sent their letters of protest to the South Carolina State government and their voices were heard; offshore drilling was fully banned in the state. The news spread like wildfire up and down the coastal states and soon North Carolina banned offshore drilling as well. It was a huge turning point and everyone was elated.

***

The day that North Carolina banned offshore drilling, Alexis lost her marbles. She had been following the legislative news blow by blow, as if each decision was a nail in the coffin of her legal career at Whyte, Farm & Bellingham. She was after all a senior associate scheduled for partnership review that autumn. And the case she was entrusted with was unraveling in front of her faster than a handful of beach sand. She was mortified.

Chandra found Alexis in the ladies room lounge chair. Alexis' mascara had smudged to wide circles around her eyes, giving her the air of a panicked raccoon. "Honey, what's going on?" Chandra kneeled down to Alexis' level and handed her a tissue. She gestured politely around her own eyes to prompt Alexis to wipe her smudged mascara.

Alexis was deeply consumed by sobs and at first couldn't get a word in. She then wiped at her eyes and nose and crumpled the tissue Chandra had handed to her. "It's all because of this damned coffee shortage!" She finally yelled out, throwing the tissue across the lounge room, which missed the trash receptacle and bounced off the wall.

"What's because of the coffee shortage?" Chandra felt bewildered by the display of anger and energy in Alexis' tissue pitch.

"I'm never going to make partner! The CTG case has fallen apart and I've been totally dysfunctional without coffee. I don't even know how this happened! I've been walking around with brain fog and I've done nothing for this case! It's all my fault!" She hid her eyes in her hand, immediately embarrassed at the outburst.

"Don't talk like that, Alexis. You're going to be fine. Come with me—let's take a break."

They walked out of Whyte, Farm & Bellingham and headed toward Two Hearts Coffee. Alexis stared at the ground and dragged her feet at each intersection, nearly stumbling over the curbs. Chandra had to make sure she got to the coffee shop in one piece.

She dropped Alexis off at a table near the corner and headed for the register. "Do you have anything with dark chocolate in it?" She asked Brigg at the counter. "This is an emergency."

Within a minute, Bring came out and brought both Alexis and Chandra two portions of Hot Mess, two spoons, and two cups of black tea. "Thank you so much." Chandra looked at him gratefully. She then encouraged Alexis to eat.

"I'm up for partnership this fall." Began Alexis after two shovel fulls of hot mess and four swigs of tea. "This case will crush me."

Chandra didn't know what to say and decided to listen.

"Do you know I'd only be the second female partner at Whyte, Farm & Bellingham? The only other woman is Sandra Devonshire, She'll be so disappointed in me!" Alexis wiped the corner of her eyes with a paper napkin.

"Was this a big project for you, Alexis?" Chandra asked.

"No! It's not even a big project. And I don't even care for it—it just fell into my lap. I've been trying to develop a practice around renewable energy. But I screwed this up, royally." Alexis blurted out dramatically.

Chandra took a sip of her tea. "Well, I can't see how you screwed it up. I mean, didn't that guy at the Port Authority take bribes and end up in the paper? And how are you supposed to know the state is going to ban offshore drilling after that happens? It seems fully out of your control."

"Yeah, but it doesn't matter. It makes me look bad!" Alexis was now biting her thumb.

"Steve, Garett, and I; and CTG — we are all in the same boat as you. And Garett is still your supervisor on this project. I just saw him this morning. He regretted the project is coming to an end so quickly, but he didn't seem too concerned." Chandra explained, leaning across the table toward Alexis. "You know, the difference between those who advance in their careers and those who do not lies in who manages to keep calm when there is

a crisis. If you want my advice Alexis, you just need to handle
this like a lady. You can't go wrong that way."

Alexis was sniffling, considering what Chandra had to say to her.
She shoveled a few more spoonfuls of the Hot Mess and drank
up her tea. "You mean I should just walz in there, pronounce
the case an unfortunate situation for CTG, and distance myself
from it?" She thought this over further. "At least I could try."

***

It was almost 3 pm when Chandra and Alexis returned to the
office. Chandra went to check on Steve and Alexis went straight
to Garrett's office, her managing partner and supervisor.

"I have some bad news for you, Alexis." Garett addressed her
gravely before she mustered the courage to broach the topic of
CTG. "You've really been very patient with this CTG project.
And I can imagine it hasn't been an easy one.... Now there's
been a bribery scandal with the Port Authority..."

Alexis interrupted Garrett before he could finish. "I heard about it and I'd like to call an impromptu meeting at the Harbor conference room with you, Steve, and Chandra."

Garrett looked surprised, as Alexis had never made any direct requests of him before. "Sure; I'll be right there."

*

The four of them sat at the glossed cherry wood table at the Harbor conference room. No one bothered with the water or the herbal coffee, or even pen and paper, for that matter. Alexis looked over at Chandra, who nodded in support.

"I understand that all of you have heard about the Port Authority scandal at this point." Alexis mustered up her best lawyer persona. "My advice based on my assessment of this case is that we withdraw from representing CTG. I value our collective expertise as a team and I believe we need to think about our reputations going forward."

Steve had personally felt done with CTG for some weeks, and did not even acknowledge the relative novelty of Alexis' idea.

But he did sense an opportunity. "We do make a good team and we'll continue to do so. I agree with Alexis that we shouldn't waste our energies here." He then realized he knew nothing about what else Alexis was working on and felt at a loss for words.

Thankfully Garrett filled in the details. "I know you're putting in a lot of work into developing a renewable energy practice, Alexis. I and the other partners were discussing the topic earlier today and we think the scandal is an opportunity to get some of our wind energy clients in front of the Port Authority. We'd like you to take the lead on that."

Alexis' face lit up and her jaw muscles seemed to relax. "I'd be happy to do that, Garrett." She replied with growing confidence.

"Steve and I would be happy to support you in any way we can, Alexis." Chandra leaned forward with a soothing tone.

Steve, feeling out of his element, looked from Alexis to Chandra and back to Alexis again. He decided the best thing to do would be to nod in agreement. "Yeah…any way we can." He finally pronounced.

***

Later that week, Steve gave Troy a call. "Troy, I'm going back to New Jersey."

"That means you're finished with your project?" Asked Troy.

"Yes; that appears to be the case." Announced Steve, recalling the events of the past week, wishing he could share the details with Troy. He suppressed the thought and instead asked, "Can I still get some ginseng tea from you?

"Thanks to you, my friend Randy started selling ginseng tea online. It's been a very popular product for him. You can get it directly — his website is printed on the bag of tea I sold you."

"Okay; I got it." Steve was holding up the nearly empty bag as he spoke to Troy. He put the bag down and searched his mind. "Troy?"

"Yes Steve?"

"I just want to thank you." Steve volunteered in a rather subdued manner.

"Thank me? For the tea? Well, you were just in luck that I had the right connections for you." Responded Troy. He thought about the price of the tea on Randy's website in contrast to what he had received from Steve for the ginseng with a twinge of guilt.

"Thanks for the tea—it was very helpful. But I mean, thank you for all the advice you gave me — you know, about dealing with that colleague? It made a big difference in the outcome of my case."

"You're very welcome!" Troy perked up enthusiastically. "And I have to thank you, too."

"How's that?"

"You encouraged me to host mindfulness classes for coffee addicts. So I did it. It's been a huge success! I'm planning to transition to teaching mindfulness full-time by the end of the year. My Buddhism instructor is helping me get my business up and running."

***

The following Monday, Chandra and Steve shared a cab ride to
the airport.

"Do you think we'll be back here again, Chandra?" He asked,
studying her profile.

"I think there's a lot of opportunity here for us with Whyte, Farm
& Bellingham and their renewable energy work." She looked out
the window.

Steve thought about this in silence. He then started tapping the
fake leather upholstery with his fingers. "Do you want to go back
to that bar next time we're both in town?"

"What bar?" Chandra asked absentmindedly, watching
Charleston Bay.

"You know, the one with the fresh squeezed grapefruit drinks?"
He asked, trying to remember the name of the place.

"Oh, the cocktail bar." Stated Chandra. "Sure."

Steve sat back in his seat, feeling very content.

Chapter 25: Out to Sea

Marie finished writing a memo to SOS headquarters about the moratoriums on offshore drilling in the Atlantic and closed her laptop. She was worried. She had been hired to work on the Oil Free Oceans Campaign and the campaign was no longer needed. What would happen to her job? She would, at least, represent SOS' interests in the remainder of the ocean planning process. But then what?

Marie took a walk through town to think about this. She could look for another position with SOS, but that might take her to another state. She didn't want to go. She really liked Brigg and felt like they were just starting to form a relationship. She also liked Charleston and the people she had met.

Not sure what she was going to do but feeling resolute, Marie found herself walking in the direction of Two Heart's coffee. It was almost five in the afternoon and Brigg would be closing up shop. Her mind wandered to Roman Ferrari as she walked. Did his kidnapping have anything to do with the SOS Oil Free Oceans Campaign? Or something to do with the coffee shortage? And why was he released into a dumpster without any demand for a ransom? She felt frustrated that she could not have done anything more for Roman.

Then there was John Warren over at the Demson University Lab. Did he have anything to do with the coffee mold situation or was her chance meeting of him a mere coincidence in her investigation of Roman's kidnapping? The harder Marie thought the less clear her thoughts became. She could feel her brain going into overload trying to make sense of the connections.

Marie decided to let go of these thoughts, focusing on her intuitive feelings about the prior months. Doing this, Marie had a vague sense that she had been a minor character in some strange series of orchestrated events by forces largely unknown to her and that were completely out of her control. She sighed as she neared Two Heart's Coffee and cleared her mind before walking in.

"Hey Marie. I heard about your success getting a moratorium passed! I bet you didn't expect to be that effective!" Brigg greeted her.

"I admit, I'm totally blown away." She responded. Then she started helping him put away some coffee mugs.

Brigg dried his hands and came over to her, a glass in hand, leaning one arm on the counter. "Marie, why don't we go out on a real date? Where we don't have to do anything for SOS or the coffee shop. Let's just do something fun together."

She looked at him while resting her chin on her hand. "I'd like that very much. How about we start by walking over to the water?"

They closed up the coffee shop and walked toward the seawall at the harbor. They looked out to the distant landform of Fort Sumpter across the glittering expanse of the bay and imagined the open ocean beyond. A wind gust blew off the water sending a breeze of cool air across their faces. Brigg wrapped his arms around Marie, resting his chin on the back of her shoulder. A myrtle leaf fell into her hair and lingered for a moment before it was carried away by the wind.

***

John Warren sat on a beach chair with his feet soaking in the water outside his new Costa Rican home. He wasn't fully moved in yet, but had shipped some of his belongings over from South Carolina. He planned to transition full-time to the tropics within the next month, but had to go back to the States one more time to help Jamie transition to his role as the new principal investigator of the research lab.

He slathered extra sunscreen on his nose and tipped a Cuban boater hat over his eyes so that he could read the newspaper he had picked up at the airport for his flight over. He unfolded the paper and read the headline, 'Governors of Southern Atlantic States Agree to 50-Year Moratorium on Offshore Drilling.' "Hmm…" he mumbled to himself somewhat impressed and then kept looking. He had heard the lab would be in the paper today. There it was, in the bottom right corner, 'South Carolina University Making Headways in Solving Coffee Mold Infestation.' John smiled in satisfaction.

No one would have to know that John had personally infected the coffee supply with aggressive coffee mold that he genetically engineered at the research lab. John had taken a big risk, gambling that Jamie's coffee mold experiments and the lab's reputation for managing tobacco plants over the decades would put them in a position to step in to save the day. It was worth the gamble. And the only way to make his retirement in Costa Rica within reach.

John had arranged a special contract with the University, giving him a hefty finder's fee for the coffee mold grant, in exchange for an early retirement package. The finder's fee breathed life into John's IRA and allowed him to finally draw a closing chapter to his career.

Now a sudden uncomfortable twinge in his sternum pricked at him at the thought of Marie Alpern. By sheer coincidence she had turned up at his lab. What was the connection again and how had she found him? Roman Ferrari had been kidnapped and suddenly he was a suspect. And then she started asking about the coffee mold and the University's contract. He had hardly slept the days after she had visited. Would the FBI check into his financial affairs and catch his lie? He felt nervous, thinking about his last and final trip planned to the US. Would he be apprehended? And was he safe in Costa Rica? He had to believe that he was.

He put the paper down and breathed deeply. The warm moist salty air caressed his skin and filled his nostrils. He looked out toward sea and fixed his eyes on the endless horizon. Forcing all uncomfortable thoughts out of his mind, he said to himself. "This is what life is about! " He got up from his beach chair and began wading in the water.